Darling

Darling

A novel by

WILLIAM TESTER

ALFRED A. KNOPF   NEW YORK   1991

WITH LOVE,
THIS BOOK IS FOR DEL AND JOSEFA

I WOULD VERY MUCH LIKE TO THANK JANE AND HEYWOOD
HALE BROUN, PEN, AND THE AUTHORS LEAGUE FOR THEIR
ASSISTANCE. MY WARMEST THANKS TO PETER CHRISTOPHER,
DIANE WILLIAMS, AND TO SERGEANT KENNETH TESTER, USAF.

*And God made the beast of the
earth after his kind, and cattle after
their kind, and every thing that creepeth
upon the earth after his kind: and
God saw that it was good.*

—GENESIS 1:25

*Farm boys wild to couple
With anything   with soft-wooded trees
With mounds of earth   mounds
Of pinestraw   will keep themselves off
Animals by legends of their own*

—JAMES DICKEY

Darling

The Killers

How can I remember her all at once when what I want is to forget? My sin, her hide against my body—God, our lives.

"Hey, Bub. Hey, look it, baby brother. Son, you never did jig our cow?" he says.

Of Darling, parts in memory is how she comes to mind, my pet, our bossy, dappled doll. We had us milking after school. We had the garden's weedy vista. There were summers we would cool all day in shade beneath our trees, a grated sun chipped in the oak leaves; some were nights when gunshot lightning rang the barn tin overhead, the rafter's roof rats bending shadows through the stall on us alone. Us love-locked, straddled on her bucket, foamed and blue-white in the straw.

So what do I picture remembering Darling?

Her gentle doe-eyed feeding nod, the lathered musk, her tender hooves.

"Say, Bubba, who was baby's only special love?" my brother says, tricked out in sailor black and hatted, bored on shore leave, such is Jeab. He has these duffel things and stuff. Jeab sets his NAVY-decaled briefcase on the table near my gun. "This piece of shit is all you got?" he says. "This play-toy here's a pistol?"

Dear Lord God.

Jeab visits, speaking to his beer across the tablecloth from me, through cans and cigarettes and litter, past our trash-surrounded years.

Now I'm here with her and Jeab again. She poses in my kitchen, broad and bovine in the sink light. See her here? She is clear an instant, nuzzled up in my pretend.

"She always did jig me best," Jeab says.

Did she with him when we were kids?

Did she do him the way that I had her?

When I was small, I used to live inside my body. I would put my arm outside and hold it to the light, and even then, our cow was there. We walked our stall like in a shell back then.

I remember when I would go looking for her—and the dark of the nights in the wind on our barn—and when Darling would look back at me.

Heaven.

What is my memory of Darling?

"You did what?" I say to Jeab.

Child

See my brother and my mother and me in the light in our
backyard, out by the barn and the silver silo rocketed up
above the barn, here on the farm of what is all there is in
the world in my mind? All there is is towered arching toward
our barn, it seems to me, small on the grass below the boards
of the bone white fence in our backyard. "See the cowy-
cow?" my mother leans and says to me; she tugs me stood-
up to her skirt front. "Come, and see the pretty cow?"

Darling looms like something giant in a book of scary
tales. She rubs her rump against the waxy stick of a china-
berry tree beside the barn, making the batch of the leaves
on the tree to shake, and some to fall like feathers all around
her and a bantam hen with chicks at Darling's hooves, our
buckskin mare off in the stall muck. Darling is liable to fall
on me and crush me on the grass, I think: our lawn has
sparkling shards of wet which shine lit on each grass blade
dewed and green up to our cow. I look up at her—and all
there is—as if from in a pit, our cartoon yard framed on
the livestock, our white fence chalked on the sky, and on
the barn, its window square and blackly yawing, tugs of

straw pinched out between the splitted boards and corners of the shipwreck of our barn.

I have lost a shoe back on the lawn. I trudge, I limp.

My mother lifts me up off of the grass. She crooks my head up and lowers my butt so I can see what all there is here at the fence behind our house: our horned young cow, the barn, and farther out, our ribbed and clodded fallow field in furrows broke and barren, the swollen tractor in it coupling something, backwards, buggish, rusted-toothed, and over all of this, the leaning, siloed, hard and cloudless hood of unimportant blue.

Darling lumbers close to us, so big-eyed and alive and like a giant toy to me, her coloring in map shapes whorled with mottled black and white. She gives my little arm a sniff; she rubber-noses me wet a bit, and I can feel the warmth of Darling's breath across my face.

This fine young cow hums out a moo into our lives.

Amongst the urchin fence-post grass, my brother finds a peach-tree limb he scratches onto Darling. Swording air between the boards, Jeab drags his limb across her horns and lifts an ear flap with his scratcher. "Yah, old cowy-cow," my brother says, and jabs her freckled eye with it.

And see how Darling stands as still as a picture of a cow caught in the light in our backyard?

In Bed

A cow, or horse, or bigger something, shovels with its hooves out in the ground around our house, or in the field—their hulking forms—beside our night yard in the dark. I wake to dark and see my hand there on my pillow like an egg, and think that cows are in our yard again; I imagine fence boards cast, or stoven in, our cows upbloated, munching on the nightmare of our lawn.

My sleeping world is being chewed on, eaten small. My newest shirt and shower towel drape like a ghost hung from my chair, in the drowning dawn.

I'm in our bunkbeds, I remember, newly twelve—and dull into a pinchful dream all terrible with school. A rainy air is in our bedroom, morning air, a Southern dampness.

Daddy's morning voice is out our door, sketching sounds, "You all," and then, "Get up." His voice becomes a long-armed, overcasting thing in my dream, in the world of how it is when I am almost all awake, when I can't move, when I am scrunching small up in my bed, my mind a nub inside my body, dull and senseless, lost and dumb, as if a little spirit-me were swimming fished within my head. My brother's bunkbed grunts above me, winding springs up in his bunk, his netted mattress hump pressed down at me; my brother breathes awake, pretending sleep. *I know he is.* Our loosened cows or something bigger hoove the ground, pick at and claw the grassy earth; they hoove to shovel up the dirt around the covers on my foot.

It seems our house, the chair, our cattle—all there is, wants us at school. I'm not afraid; it's just the closet. Clomping gallop pumps our pasture. In my bedroom, whispers talk. Like in our shower stalls in gym that laugh like air caught in the faucet. Shirted nothings in our closet nod and mutter, watch, they see.

Outside our room my daddy knocks his weighty hand against the door.

"Boys," he says.

Jeab pushes at the air and hits the floor, bumping looser laid-out odds and ends, and on our desk, coins, pens, nails shelved in the wall all tremble gently, clatter, ring. Jeab brings his shadowed legs before me in this strip of doorcrack light in our dark room. "Hey, Bub, get up," my brother says. "Son, hit the deck." Here stands the black and polished marble of Jeab's body in the dark. As Jeab is pulling up his pants, he trunks his bending cock above his underwear elastic, leaves our room into the bare and glaring lightbulb of our hall, his morning business in the bathroom pealing brightly through the walls.

I still have to close my eyes, and make as if to clear my throat, and cough. I'm near asleep.

I have to make a fuss with me to get myself to school. The seventh grade is like some bullies waiting, ganged up in the halls.

The coming day sends me its pictures: us out feeding in the barn, us in the cracked seats of our class and in the showers after gym—the shower boys with me and Jeab undressed, the shower waters on.

I see the splashing shower boys about like horses wet and fine.

When I try to remember things that year, she reappears. At times, this year runs in a circle in my head, a yellow necklace strand of days which flit and pass to flash again.

I see her grazing in the rain light in our pasture in the day.

I help my brother rush our chores before we hop our bus to school.

Here, Jeab and I are growing up.

Mornings, Mama has her grits and blackened gravy biscuit done. She's smoking menthols in our kitchen with her waitress apron on. In standing rows, wallpapered flowers near the ceiling blur with stain, from smoke, or grease, or leaking water, wilted old. A brace of okra on the counter soak afloat in Mason jars, my mama's sampler on the stove wall: *They are rich who have true friends.* I have my place beside her at the table with my eggs; across from me, my brother absent in his math book, scratching signs. His Christian name rhymes with the "King" marked on his ruler, giantly. My mama coughs her cigarette and pours us coffee in our sweet milk. Mama's face does like she studies something held up to her nose, her squinted, drowsy, sewing stare. Her nose and mine hook much the same: we share her face's family shape, but hers has deeper places, power, flecks of powder in her skin.

I'll stand there quiet in our bathroom, Mama's face around my mind. Alone, I'll try to do her smile and make myself turn into her, me smiling, dolled up in the mirror with her lipstick slid on me.

I'll kiss her cool and mirrored image.
Leave a lip print red with wax.
"You all eat up now, Bub," she says.
I make like I'm too wrecked to eat. My mama's eggs
have too much grease for me; my gravy biscuit's bottom
part is blackened into hard. Everything is grabby-like and
pinching at my eyes. Everything's too big and glared to see,
each noisy thing cupped in our kitchen mean with sitting
here and fuss—I want to throw shit through the windows,
crawl up tucked in Mama's aproned lap and rock off back
to sleep. I put a wiggly blistered bacon in my mouth the
taste of salt.

We're getting niblet close to harvest, working late at
early crops. We're crating butternuts and mustard. Hired
coloreds load the trucks. Way after dark we tend to livestock, milk and feed. We bathe and eat.

At times, I'll slip off in the midnight, gone in me. I'll dog
our lawn. Larger, me out in my darkness, in our cow lot
haunting things.

But now is how we are here in the country in our house;
every one of us is dead.

Each year we're closer, Daddy cusses us, to losing every
worthless speck of all we ever had.

He tries, but we can't run our farm.

My daddy comes into the kitchen with his Stetson in his
hand—which sort of twitches at the brim like in a dream.
The lines of sleep scrim up my daddy's face when Daddy
sees it's me. He hangs his Stetson on his chair. My daddy
hasn't slept enough for him to be awake; he isn't ready yet
for playing with us. Everyone is foggy save my brother in
his math. Jeab's leaf-rubbed hands will not wash clean. I
fold back from breakfast, shut my eyes, and pull my neck.
My head rolls on a flimsy spring, and Daddy asks if I am
feeling poorly much this morning. Says, "You boys aren't

fishing trouser trouts when you all got your school, are you?"

Mama clicks her cheeks at him, then covers her mouth with her cigarette hand and grins. "Lord, Joe, if you'll not have them ruined."

I fork a lava flow of yolk; I bow my wooden dolly head.

"You reckon we're not already been?" Jeab says. "Old Bub's looking short of fuel."

The ornery leghorn in our henhouse caws a rooster call for feed. I hear its wings slap on the wall tin, rattled things.

"—You think he'll live?" Jeab grins and yanks my sleepy ear.

I make my iron face at him. Tired, I was too late out last night, amongst our sleeping cows. I swear there's more to be afraid of every day just being seen.

"You all behave," my daddy says. My daddy once was small as us—I see his shrunk and younger self, shy in a chair, at Grandpa's house. "Well, boy, if you're still feeling puny, best as you should stay inside." I nod yes to him, and Daddy, he tells Jeab to finish crating in the squash and not be bothering me today.

I saw Jeab dancing in our shower water naked in the steam.

"Hey, Bubba, check this mother out!" he said.

The monster of his cock between his shower-watered legs.

I turned and toweled into my corner where I washed hid off from Jeab.

I want to bash my brother's head in. Scoop my spoon into his perfect eyes and blind him, grinning here. I think my brother might read my mind.

"Like I did what?" is what Jeab says, facey.

Jeab says what did he do, anyway, and biscuits at his plate. Mama combs her hand back of my neck, then takes her hand back to her coffee cup. "Now shush," my mama says to my brother Jeab.

"You stay in bed like Daddy says. Now love your mom."

I kiss her chin.

"Don't you be up and playing none," she says.

Nothing of this morning seems to *fit*, is what it is. I drink some coffee-colored milk, and go and crawl on in my bed.

I con my way around my family; sneaking, here I am back then, fidgets, skelety with headaches, damp and scrawny greenish legs. I fear a razorblade, our showers, and the coming seventh grade.

Our yellow bus pulls in out front. Talk is outer-doored and in our yard, then our truck, then there is nothing but the rooster and some cows around our house, and me alone, kneeing curled up in a pocket God would have across his shirt, his clouding breath wrapped on my bed against the monsters arming back, and our old house is full of haunts that come when we go off to school, and I am here with God alone and all there is, me in small up in my bed, me and God on our farm of the whole, wide world.

Nothing feels as good to me as this does, bedded here.

I'm not growing any older.

I am never getting out of bed or off our farm again.

White Fence

Outside, we have a white gate with a trellis over it knitted through with wetted rose limbs on the fence, between the barn and the scraped junkscape of our brown yard; I can see out from my bed onto the windowed afternoon. My bed, of the lower of the bunkbeds, thick with covers. My breath mists on the window in a smudge, then clears into a watered lens I wipe around the day. I lick our gate out in the daylight in the noon inside the lens.

Something in our living room ticks, or something with its footsteps settles resting on the wood, and like a ghost, it bumps the air down the shadow of our hall walls into my shoebox bit of room. Then I hear the tick again as a memory in my head, as if the ghosts or creeping devil conjured somewhere in our house, the nightmare him I feature real and almost see. I hear the almost soundless roaring of the quiet in the air. Our house is holding its breath, it seems, all swollen to the walls. Outside are ponds of mud and rainy wet still on the ground. Tin lifts in the wind out on the roof of our red barn, settles slow. Whistles coil around our house.

On stirring dressed to go outside, I come to the hallway by their door, a painted Jesus on our knickknack shelf of photos in the hall. The deer-leg coat rack on the end wall. Warped linoleum molds our floor.

We're poor as yard dirt, Mama says, in this old shed. Our town is citrus groves and crackers, marsh and cattle, land of sun. We have our church on up the road, our store, the hopeful green of pastures, shacks, a skullish gutted truck beside some house all boarded up, its patched or glassless, blackened windows roofed in tin bled through to rust, and the fallen lawns.

The beaned catalpa in our yard, magnolia, Spanish moss and sawgrass and the trunks of clay-road palm trees in our evenings gone to pink.

I find my mama and daddy's room is curtained blue in their window light. Even all their furniture looks blue. The heavy smell of Mama and Daddy is like the smell of hangered clothes, of dampened collars, and of darkened, closet smells. A spongy, spraycan, laundry smell of something powdery and lead. A wall of Mama's smell wells up above my mama and daddy's bed—of Mama's hair, or of a towel that has been used, of talc, and then my daddy's thinner smell in under hers. Daddy's smell is bitter; it lingers edged and orange peelish, sweated, lifting from their bed.

This is Daddy's hard desk chair, and him, or just my sense of Daddy haunted on the vinyl in the dimness in their room. I feel him. See how broad his rear has worn the pattern from the chair—the size of Daddy on the seat!

I start to think that all I look at here comes out of me somehow, as if I thought this daydream room up like a bean pressed from my head.

I hold it. Here this is, a picture.

Me remembered, still a child.

Look at it if you will.

.   .   .

Then his boy, Elroy, Jane, his wife, each day on TV shows at three. These days we watch our gray cartoons until our daddy drives up home. We run. Or put ourselves to work. I make like sick, get in my bed.

My daddy's anger in our house, his pressure swelling in the rooms wherever Daddy stews or is. A spidered thing around my father feeds the angry up in him. So we get scared. I guess I hide.

I take my life out to our cow. To Darling.

"Who was baby's only favorite one?" my brother said.

Sometimes I'll treasure through their drawers—I'm slinking; I'll ease back the drawer of Mama's perfume-cluttered bureau: a paper box, a lotion tube, this lip-print tissue ball, and there are things that they have hidden in a place that moves around, hid from the closet to the bureau, to the closet back again. Here, a band with snaps in black elastic, here a wrap of cellophane from something. Under clothes back in her drawer there coils the rubber length of hose, the belted girdle cooling folded, mussy scarves, her rubber bulb. Mama's drawer has a sort of shoe-store smell of wads and knots of slickened cloth. Her dim and tangled cocoa hose; her clouded silks and nylons stretch, then grit against themselves and catch the splintered cedar board inside my mama's chest of drawers. Here lies a fog of nylon stocking toeing brown around my arm. I move some silk on silk of something between my finger and my thumb, inhale it wadded to my face and smell the wash. My heart throngs like a fever with the blueness on my skin. Hot is mostly up my arms and on my shoulders and my neck. I hear a car go by our house, outside, that does not sound like ours. I know God, or God and something else is watching in the dark. I sit down across their cottoned bed.

I lay myself on back.

Darling

. . .

I'll sin myself and think of Kay: at Grandpa and Grandma's house, my cousin, Kay, lies in her T-shirt on the mattress in her room. Her watching dolls rowed on her dresser, reaching, cat-eyed wide in wonder why my arm is up her shirt. Kay's ribbing back bares on her mattress, muggy nights, her on our rug. My cousin sprawls out in our hay loft, all our cows about our barn—our loco longhorn, Midge and Molly, Sass and Cupid, Sue and Dot.

Against this bedspread Kay surrounds me, powdered window-curtain blue, her shell of ear tucked in the blondeness of her ropey golden hair. Kay once would pour across my body, her warm belly like a washcloth clutching wet onto my chest.

—I see me sneaking out in darkness in our fields to see what is.

Buttercup and Sophie. Queen.

And *Darling*.

How can I remember her all at once?

Her curving horns, her stalk of tail, my simple, cardboard cut-out cow in an ideal field.

I'll call her. Parts are how the cow comes in my mind.

I stop this mess and zip my pants, all sort of let-down, scared and done with it, and flushed a little violent. Now a car goes by our house. Some cars are always going by or it is quiet, not much else, but past the blue of Mama's bedroom with her curtains on the glass, I look for life out through the windows: no one's home, no car is there. There's just the air and me, my thinking, hid alone, at home from school.

. . .

Sometimes while lying on their bed I'll make-believe I've left my body, glassy fly inside a soda bottle crawling from my life, and times, while I am waking up, I'll dream I feel myself outside myself and bouncing up around against the ceiling of our house. I'll dream I'm floating over church or I'll be up above the ocean on the sea waves, flying me.

But I'm not growing any older, home, my mind out in my bedroom like the dust that motes our house. I pull my pole, I root, I tug myself to get myself to grow—I think that I can stretch my wiener like a carrot from the dirt.

I've wanted to grow to someone big. I've needed to be as big as him. I have the armed and leggy snake in me with Jesus in my chest.

I wish I'd grow up big like Jeab.

Later Us,
the Tablecloth

Jeab, beery, points to me his sea things with my pistol, naming shells. "She's moonwhelk, pearly abalone. Baywhort, tiger, maiden's rose. My newest favorite is corals. Look at here."

A hardened, spongy trunk of violet. On my table, bony piles.

"I found this trilobite in Norfolk on a sea wall down the quay."

He visits, sitting in my kitchen big as life, my brother, Jeab. He scoots the barrel of my gun to cull a penny from the clutter. Silver buttons on his collar show an anchor on the world.

"You got some weapons you collect or just this old, tee-tiny one?"

I say I maybe have a few.

We're here. The beer and many seashells set my table like a meal. Jeab rakes his seashells in a curve.

"Here's Indonesians, Marianas. Periwinkle, prophet's star." A pearly cluttered swirl of toffee on my gingham tablecloth.

Jeab swings off his pea coat shouldered hung across the

chair back. On one muscle, inked in green is his clawed tattoo. His Navy clothes are mostly corners, woolen black or ironed white; the medaled, particolored ribbons mark the front part of his coat. All his gold looks polished.

"Good God, what a wreck," he says. Jeab turns his emptied beer can up and takes the bottom suds, the sudsy beer drops falling measured in my kitchen's jittering light. Drops of beer in foam strobes sluicing onto my brother's tongue. Jeab presses a waist into his can and sets it rocking on the tablecloth, says "Gee-ma-fucking-netty, Bub." He grunts.

I can taste the way his breath smells in our air.

I ask Jeab does he want another cold one.

"Go ahead," he says.

Jeab shakes his hatted head at me. "So you don't give your brother a hug?" he says. "Well, God Almighty, son."

My brother thumps me in my ribs. "You think as I don't miss back then? You're simple. Lord, but what we've done."

While he is talking about our farm, Jeab hobbles, legging from his uniform, which he folds in creases, blocky, neat and flat, and puts into his duffel bag next to his chair. A welt of waistband belts the saddle of his hips; his legs are bruised. Hairless as an Amazon's, but bigger. Ham slick. Here is the butcher's chart in cuts of steak above his shins: the lumping giblets in his guts and in the sausage of his groin. The twirling furs above his groin run to his heart. Jeab stands like a swimmer in my kitchen in his shorts, and puts on jeans and a mean gray T-shirt printed *Winged Death from Above*, with a grinning skull, his arcing arms above his head like in a dive, puts on his NAV-TAC lettered baseball cap and thumb-tip bills it level squared. "I used to ride you on my bike," he says. "You wasn't but this big."

I tell Jeab we worked too much.

Jeab says he doesn't remember when.

Jeab checks his T-shirt's printed image. "Can you not tell if I'm civilian?" Jeab says, billing at his cap.

So he is here.

I see him shirtless in our pasture riding Darling in the light.

I see his arrowpoint of jet across a mentholated sky, Jeab's gleaming fighter pilot helmet chipped and fibered with the sun.

Here are steaks and chops and fat cuttings parceled. Jeab has the Adam's apple of some unlikely lizard working swallows in his throat, the dappled freckles on his neck fanning dotted as an apple where the apple stem goes in. Jeab says, "They don't let me fly my sidearm out on leave. What other guns you got around?"

I tell Jeab I did my part when we were kids.

"Yeah, son, get real," my brother says. "What's in the fridge?"

Jeab opens my refrigerator door, and I can hear the motor miss, trundle a moment, stop running. Jeab looks in my refrigerator, sideways then, at me.

"It's nothing but some beer in here. And a egg." Jeab says. "Now, how're we going to put a little pudding on the runt? Huh, son?"

Jeab says, "My God, but you ain't scrawny. You don't drink?"

Outside my kitchen window it starts to rain. A wetted dark spot on the glass, and then another blotting spot, and then some smaller dark spots mar the glass, and water pops outside of my apartment—you can hear it falling larger then, and rain is dropping dark on things in tip-tap separate sounds out in the city's purple night. I tell my brother we can still go out. Jeab says he doesn't feel *that much* like dressing just to eat. He sweeps his seashells in a sandwich bag.

"Well, we can order in," I say.

"My daddy beat the hell out me."

And I don't disagree.

He lived the bad end of the stick, Jeab being big when we were kids.

Jeab never played.

Monster

Another day when I'm alone, winter, shit froze into biscuits
crisp below our powdered sky, an oyster white with muddied
sunlight, on the morning, lazy me. I hang the milk I've pulled
from Darling, shake her straw, and drop my clothes. The
clouding cold is like a pillow on our mattress of the straw,
a smell of mice and rotted cabbage, smells of cow and cow
manure and my skin about the stall—I have that sour,
mouthy smell where I have licked my skinny arm. I brunt
her haunches good apart, and push her naked with my shoulder at her quarters so she'll give, my face a smudge against
her hide, the oil and rooted smell of cow. I love my doll.
I'll make my forts all day with her. I feel my stool sink down
against where Darling's hocks are elbowed back, her knee
joints warped and bending wrong-wayed, soft and backwards as a bird's, her strap of gone-inside-her tail. Her tail
is knuckled up with bones and whisking rope ends at the
end. I cow-step wiggly on my stool; I heft her tail.

Her conch shell. Hide split like a mango is her place
behind my cow. Her place, like something from the water,
something plopped beneath the ocean shelled and shapeless

on a rock. She looks like that, well, more or less. I pet and stroke my chest at her.

To noonlight. Sparrows find our window, fluff their feathers—see us, fly. I have to spit on us to get us both bespawled. I'm knobbing, *horror* with a hard-on like an arm between my legs, but smaller, wiener-sized and fisted like this knob come from my body is some awful baby's arm.

Some monster.

Now I get on in.

A pigeon falls before the window on the world around our stall. It dudders, Jesus and the devil flapping batlike at the sky.

I put myself behind of her.

I plug my awful hard-on in this sweetly feeding doll.

I pull her rubber folds apart and put myself in hers.

"Don't say anything."

"Don't say anything to Mama about the cow," I say to Jeab.

Our mother: "You all come wash up!" she said.

"So who was baby's only special love?" is what Jeab says.

Her gentle doe-eyed feeding nod, the lathered musk, her tender hooves.

Parts are how our love comes to my mind.

I go to Doll.

Fire Night

Then here is Daddy kissing Jeab, and then my daddy kissing
me; he crushes me up in his arms and swoops me lifted by
my waist like I am just a sack of feed across this car hood
of his shirt back. Here's his belt, a bit of yard, our garden's
hothouse, upside down. I watch the sadly drooping Christmas lights loop hope around our house, turned over; things
slip from the ground and seem to fall up to the stars on our
fired night.

Some crunkly bones pop in my chest in Daddy's solid
hairing arms—he jams me jumbling to the ground.

Now all of us watch out by the fire, mothy sparks.

I see Jeab has watered ink-run marks in gleams washed
on his cheeks: Jeab is crying, and the light thrown from the
fire shines in wet across his face. My mama hugs him; then,
like she is pouting, smacks his charcoal-sooted arm. Jeab
seems to steam against the darkness, timbers sputter, twist,
they wheeze.

Our shrinking barn sinks in a mountain of the embers
through the ground. Our barn is swallowed by the world
in a pit of flame.

My daddy kisses Jeab *and me as well*, out in the throw-down from the fire on the night. I am small, so I can let my daddy hug me more than he hugs Jeab.

So this is Christmas on our farm.

My brother, Jeab, has burned our barn down.

Cowboy

On up through spring I hide from school, their liar, hookying
at home with all the ghosts smoked in our walls, behind our
couch the elbowed devil, coughed-up hairball wads of dust
where the devil crawls in our ticking house. I dare him out
into the air and go and wrap this baby Coke along with
biscuit in my cover, on our lawn out back, the brilliant,
soddened noon. It looks like God up on our roof. The sun
has come. The rain has faded. I climb the cold antenna pole
clamped to the eave above our porch, my grip where hands
have smoothed the pole to turn the television right. As I
chin up, a startled robin flashes silent off the tiles, the scattered patchwork of the shingles in their sandy cypress green,
then standing tall, I'm larger now. I have the feeling I could
leap across the ashes of our barn, the stalls—if I could just
let go enough—the all of what there is around the junkyard
of our farm. I'm not so small up on the roof. I am out and
alive in the airy world again, my farm and me alone.

Who's home?

Old Scratch is in our attic.

There's his breath hot at my back—it seems as soon as

it gets noticed what good feeling in me goes. I spread a taint on things I'm seeing, in the daylight, fevery.

Far off are cows out anting distant in our field in black and brown. I watch, and drink my baby Coke, and burp the cakey fizz of biscuit. I'm like a doll tossed on our roof, and there are ghosts loose in our house beneath my feet against the ceiling. Fitful ghosts are in the ground—ghosts in our stalls.

Our yellow bus junks up and yaws across the blacktop county road. Inside, I see the heads of school kids in the row of window squares. I fly a crow-line way to school past all the houses and the farms, on into town, but it's not really there. Our sprawling school appears pretended, underwater, in a dream. It disappears when I'm not in it.

I glimpse the sun bent on my cousin's brassy hair, hot, gold guitar strings lifting breezy in a window of our bus, the oval, candy red of sweater, shouldered there against the glass. The little, moony-yellowed children's heads, and little, children hands.

Then here's my brother, Jeab, again. He stalks across our county road, a hero from a Bible tale, his hard jawbone in the out-of-doors. His spit there glistening on the grin on his lips. He walks past something animal the dogs dragged in our yard, a busted garbage bag, a roll of news, this shedded skin of panty hose. Up by the fence our rain-filled pinball game sits gunshot, tilted, webbed with holes, then compound buckets, crates, a plow. Some hens shit on our porch step, greenish jewels.

So Jeab is prince of all of this! I know he is. He says that this will all be his someday, and Jeab takes all of what there is of this as being his, by being older and much bigger than I'll ever get to be.

Our yellow bus junks on to miniature on down our county road.

Out front, the whining of the door spring as the screen door swings to shut.

Our many ghosts mist in the closets and the walls throughout our house, but like a cow I stay outside. I finger sand up from a shingle, sip my carbonated drink.

Once people get into the world, things fall apart, it seems to me. It's not one all-connected world, but different shrill and sharded, fretful places: back porch, yard, a raft of boards, the barn, my bit of rooftop—what was all, what all was wholeness. Jeab breaks everything to separate, small and jealous of our hearts.

Inside our house some voices clatter like our TV set is on. I hear my brother shout out, "Bub. Hey, Bub!"

But I'm not home. I'm off and feathered, flown, a robin, with my mind up in the sun.

Jeab stalks from our back porch with a folded slice of bread. "Yo, listen, Bub," my brother says, and peering distant some he looks for me and bites a hunk out of half his bread. "Hey fuck," Jeab says to nothing. "Let's get to work."

I watch the top of what is my brother's head. "I am sick," I say to him.

Jeab turns to look where I am sitting on our roof up in the sun.

"Then how's it you're now up and kicking?"

"I need sun."

"You're something. *Swear* but you're not something. Go and figure it," he says. "You need anything, Bub?"

"Yeah," I tell him.

"You okay enough to do the cows?"

Jeab puts the rest of his bread into his mouth, and munches on some sounds which hold his mouth up in his head, then like an earthquake whomps the haunted ground, he hefts his bending barbells, shrugs, and tosses them to fall.

I feel it joggle in the cinderblocks beneath our rocking house and shudder up our slatted walls on through the gable of our kitchen where a shingle grits my head. I have to hold our roof to watch. I shinny down before our house is shattered, topples, and we're crushed; and later, I will have to stay here in the wreckage as a ghost, a haunt with all the other ghosts inside our house when I'm alone.

And I will be the ghost that has to make the ticking sound.

I lay my empty bottle and my blanket on our porch, come back around to watch my brother shove his weights into the air, inhale, then blow out spirit from the blowhole of his mouth and shake the ground. No more a shirt on over my brother's chest, upwedged and heaving bellowed like a swollen heart to me. My branchy hands hung in my pockets, pots of zinnias on our porch.

He spits. I smell the sweating male of him. I watch. Jeab has a chest on him you want to lick. I can see my cousin licking at it, naked on the grass, their curling, lower adult hair shown on their bellies in the sun. I should be pushed around by Jeab, or have him mount me like a dog, have dirt or cow manure kicked on me—how dogs or bulls will do to a smaller dog or a smaller bull.

"Done . . ." he says. "You coming, Bub?"

"Better not," I say, "I have some stuff to do, milk."

"Well, I allowed as much," he says. "Is Daddy hiding anywheres?"

"No."

"Well," he says. Jeab pulls his flannel shirt back on, and foots his clinking weights back in the dust below our house, says, "No, don't get up, Bub."

My brother shakes his head at me and goes.

I sit here. "No, I won't," I say.

I walk my echoes through our house and get my bucket

and a towel. In Mama and Daddy's room, I check the look of all their things. Mama's bureau dresser looks the same, the things on it in coma. I push Daddy's chair into his desk, then pull it back. I tug at the bedspread on their bed. The devil at their bedside tugging, too, his gentle breath beside my neck. His smell, the salty smell of bread. Of shirt and wash as I walk out.

I can't stop my head.

I run some water in my bucket and go outside. Out back are puddled bogs of flood on weedy junk across our yard, a thread-bald retread tire waterlogged, mosquitoes sifting blurred, in orbit. Grayly scaled and peeling, stand our fruitless fence and trees. A crockery toilet cracked and leaning, streets of pipe rust by our yard. Our farm, like some old ruined factory give-up into the heat, and the dampened weeds.

I unlatch our gate and feel some water pat my hair, my head wetting slow, in spots of cold, the way that warm would move around my butt when I would wet my bed. I see trellis slats with paint shavings wet against the sky, the sun is low, and water runs the limbs of Mama's roses, either side of our white gate. If I ease open the gate, I know the trellis will get me soaked, so I don't. I bolt. Water falls all over me like rain. Their little water droplets falling, on our yard grass, water-clear.

I chain back the gate shut on the quiet of our yard. From up the road, my daddy's truck drives in, and gearing, throats a downshift. Daddy gets out with a feed bag, hollers, "Jeab," he hollers, "Son?" I've got my bucket just in time. My daddy will think I'm at my milking and he'll leave to go help Jeab, and then the all of what there is that is our farm will just be mine. I'll lie down drowsy in the evening wind with God and fly around, and like a rock, or like a cow, I'll never leave our littered farm. I'll go out hiding where the cows are lying down and be a cow. I'll stoop to eat the soggy grass just like a cow beside our cows. And I will sleep beside our cows, and never ride our bus to school.

I'll never step into the showers with my brother, Jeab, again, his hairy stomach, and the monster of his cock between his legs.

My boots crunch on the wax leaves of the salad grass and weeds. There are black trees on the wire fence far across our land.

Darling there looms solid large, waiting in the dark for me.

She moos.

Some nights I think Darling moos for me.

What the Thunder Said

The tint of lightning on my kitchen. Sunken rain clouds rut the buildings at the center of my town, great floating, footlit waves of cloud which take the buildings up in tide, like sandy sea forts I remember—chairs, their office walls and bodies fall pretended down the air, from here, the trucking sound of thundering and traffic on cement. Sirens.

Strangers walk by, muttering their minds into the night. *An unreal town.*

"I usually use the hollow-points, since I'm alone," I say.

"You do?"

"I mean, that is, *I would*," I say.

"Bub, you're still crazier than a pet coon. Well, fucking ay, let's have a look," he says. "We're not getting any younger. You still here?"

I see us boys up on his bike, me seated, balanced all but falling from his antlered handlebars. The push of air at us was jetting. "Hold on, Bub. Hey, Boo, hey look it, baby brother."

You still here?

I see our road run underneath of us, the black-and-white

divider feed the tire of his bike, black-white, black-white. We're here. He lives.

On through the laundry-tussled canyon of the boxes in my room, I pass my single bedroom window, silent brick stones of a building wall a yard across from mine. My window opens on a fireplace's darkened chimney stones, an oven wall, a wall lit ashy, black and glowing from the lives lived down below. Their single lamplit lower window lights my air shaft dustily, with smoke, or dust-filled yellow gasses, citied tiredness and smog. Soft Spanish radioing songs come through the walls.

"¿Dónde vas? ¿Dónde has estado?"

"You ever miss when we was kids?" he says, his words called from the kitchen thrown like pillows down my hall.

I miss, remembering her stillness. Me in her.

Then I get cauled up in the blankets and the boxes in my closet, gently tottering a hanger with its hook necked from a shroud: my hooded jacket in its rocking nods accusingly at me. It saunters waiting to be taken: sometimes searching for a shirt, a piece of clothing chooses me. One chair is perfect for a moment, flirting, some small patch of grass mossed in the park wants me to lie—my closet door shuts at my back. It nudges, closing me inside against my squawking rack of clothes in the drapey dark.

Frisk through my closet for the shoebox. There, the sack of violet velvet hiding minnow shapes of lead, a sack that once someone had liquor in with a drawstring at the top, but now my hand reaches in under the shoebox lid like your hand in a hole for a chick, or a cat, or a lobster in a hole, or your hand in a closet in the dark. Or a heart. In the sack are the hollow-point slugs, and the heavy of lead in my hand is the center of the closet somehow, as if lead had done science to the air in this dark.

My brother, "God were we a sickness, tipping cows out in the barn."

We'd ram our sleeping-solid cows. They fell. Their legs gave as if murdered as their tons rocked to the ground.

I crunch my grape-colored sack on the tablecloth, and sit down across from Jeab. It is raining outside by the street-light's bloom, in city-blown gustings of rain. "This .22 could use a pin," I say.

Now Jeab and I in my kitchen alone, my window and the rain. Outside, the water falls in sequins, in the streetlight rainy strings. A sticking leaf canoes my window.

Jeab waves with the pistol by its grip, then holds it flat across the tablecloth. "Yeah, used to fuck our 4-H calf . . . The shit we did back then."

I sip my beer and look at him. "You're kidding, Jeab. For real?"

Jeab says, "No lie, you should of seen."

So where was Jeab while I was milking? Where was he? *Hey, Boo. Hey, look it, baby brother.*

I try, but I can't take my brother. I hold on, but this won't ride.

Outside, the lightning through my window blues like dawn lit on our night.

"Now, you did what?" is all I say.

Three Dogs

What is my memory of him, of Jeab, of the plunderer, pillager, Indian king, with his gun in the wintery dark by our rat-mobbed barn? Jeab wears his jeans, his mackinaw jacket, and a deer-hunting cap on his head.

Of the gunman marauder, the cop and the cowboy, gone-eyed Jeab? Stone killer, USN lieutenant, and a Jeab as a hero, the prince, and the terror, a hunter of dogs.

We slip out nights to do our playing, armed, will spit out with machine-gun noises, kill ourselves at war. This one night, Jeab draws back the white door of our barn—its rafters swarmed, our scattered rats trapped by the light lit like a party on inside, or an ark with the smell of some cows and some pigs and some horses and some mules and some chickens and some guineas and some peahens and some sheep having a party in the ark, but inside it is a jumping bed of hay, and the light of a house, or a party going on. A yellowy light full of dust on the hay, and no animals now, but the three mange dogs wired tight to the beam at the center of the barn Jeab would burn.

Its back is a brush on the black standing dog, as if braced for a push from a truck, or to water in a tub, and the gray-spotted dog has a mouse of some hair on the beam where the dog maybe rubbed, and the mouth of this dog shows some milk. It peers back and forth looking up, and tied next to it is the sleepy-looking dog, as if lying down calm from a nap, or a dog that is thinking there is nothing much wrong when my brother throws down with his gun. Jeab is posed—like he knows he is watched as he aims. Like a Jeab who *pretends* he is aiming a gun, like a boy playing war with a toy.

Then the black standing dog snatches air in its chops and a slaver of milk strands the air.

Air claps a slamming of sound—it roars, a gunshot torn like lightning walks a limb into our barn, the shattered hay bits drift and settle, riding lightbeams rimmed with noise. Our barn is hammer-waved in ringing. Chirr and trilling. Crickets sing.

I flinch. The shotgun's second roar.

Mama calls us from the porch, says, "What's going on, yonder?"

"You all come wash up!" Mama yells. Till this is what my memory has of her.

We lived with Mama on our farm back then when nothing had an ending, no end came. No place where I could say, *This winter ends*. There mostly just were pictures. Some things happened. Mostly things were still in the watching dark.

There weren't any stories. Almost everything is missing here, of her.

I took my turn. Hitler. Dillinger. The evil us, at hide-and-seek at night. We snuck our play.

Her

Outside in the night, egged-in under the moon-shadowed snake of the blackened trees that line the fence around our farm, cattle lie, still and breathing, whitely cow shapes, pale white as breasts, or as stones butting from a graveyard in the dark on this cold March ground. My toes are ice cubes in my shoes. The black of trees across the lighter dark where night is looms. Alive-looking, like in a book of monsters. Our trees are like some cloud-large snake with all our bedded cows inside, which turns and maybe hisses, yawns, and sucks up all there is around our small and sleeping farm—and I am swallowed in the night.

Out by a block of almost unseeably dark cow she lies, pale as a wash on a line at night. As I move through the shade of the fence-line trees, I smell, sauced-in, on tines of cold, her cow-manure smell, and something else, burst or cut or soured weed cuttings, oak, acorn, old milk—the straw and cow-manure smell of cow. Cows outside on the grassless sandlot, bedded down in dark. This night is how and where, and all about, the stuff that Darling is.

Look.

Darling slowly turns into a papier-mâché cow shape in

the drawn night-curtaining. Cool, blue-white as milk, as still
and as patient as sheep. Now she is, vividly: her horns, her
pointed-down bone-wedge head, white-shanked legs, her
huge night coloring.

Darling there, is always waiting quiet in the dark for me.
She tongues my arm for feed.

"Whoa now, girl," I say to her, and head her for the
stall. It's just us two out in the dark, this me and her.

We stop at a block of hay in the corral behind the barn,
and I snap Darling's lead onto her halter ring. She nods back
to give resistance just a little, mostly show. Her evening
visit's bit of temper. My end of the lead is around a post. I
pat Darling's withers, feel her hide twitch on my palm—
weirdly sprung, a hide electric as a horse at shying bugs. I
guess she doesn't want the lead snapped on.

When looking at the ground, when Darling noses into
sorrel, reddish herb, the sweet alfalfa lawning greenly on
our field, does she have something in her head that tells her,
This is weed, or *This is grass*? Is there a picture in her head,
or is the surface all she sees?

Sometimes I hear a young me talk, a surer, tougher me,
sometimes. It's like a *truer* me were up inside me running
things.

I spread out and fluff some hay for us inside the stall,
covering the stall muck of this morning with a rough and
thickly haying blanket. Shots of flies skit in the curtained
flashlight air, cloud-thick. I shake feed in Darling's trough,
and lead her in, then close the gate behind on us.

A sour of piss and rotted cream the smell of vinegar or
metal. There's her smell of sour beer. I have the flashlight
on the nail. Down underfoot, a rotted rat or guts, or squishing pound of burger, her manure in the straw. I tie her lead
in through her feed trough, leg my stool up close to Darling
at her ilium, where it dents.

"Come on, get your leg up, girl."

Darling munches at her feed again.

Well, this is how you milk a cow. Head in, with a rhythm of rowing an Indian canoe, the floaty duck, the slow, enormous heron birds, teal blue and winging off a pond's flat water. Elbows lower than my knees, pressing the all of me, until Darling, letting loose her milk, presses the bulk of the barrelous, swollen all of her back at me; we are a balancing act.

I sort of turn it in my hand, like this, like so. One, and then another teat, like my thing is. Squirting her.

Just her milk, my breath. Like so. Like this is all the world inside our barn. The flashlight causes straws to shadow straw shapes on the boards along the stall walls.

And Darling moos.

The warm from pushing her—my head caps leatherly in the pillow of her haunch. The warm spots on my knees dig in her flank and in her bloated, punchball stomach. Hear the water run in Darling like my brother's stomach does when he is going at his weights, or by our TV on the floor. That gurgle, blood and milk in her. I watch the milk strand in my bucket, squirts of milk which strup the zinc and make the sound of when I milk, and Darling's milk is rising foamed like Daddy's shaving cream will do—or like the milk that clabbers sweet and icing white in whipping cream, the crunching, wooden sounds of foam.

And I am lost inside the white.

While milking long, I close my eyes. I feel my bones slip in the muscles of my lost-in-working arms. I'm swimming sightless in the deep up in her milk; I'm lost in dark down in a hole, like parts of sleep: I'm kind of gone.

I see naked squirming every girl I know up in the clouds; I get hard and think of Jeab, of Kay and Jeab out on our rug. I hook my half-full bucket high away up on a nail.

Darling

It starts with fishing in my trousers—ends again, me in my sinning, fine and stripped at jerking off a bit. My sunned and little pocket frog, and my heart in its powered heat.

As I do drummings on my stomach, me, the wind does whistled mouth sounds on the stall. I see my mama and my cousin and some teachers in our school, our school bus driver on the bus with me, her breasts bared on the straw and on my mama and daddy's turned-down bed in blue there in their room, the cottoned, cooler white of pillows on the bedspread at the head, and Daddy's smell and sense of him, with her about the room, haunting it, *the stuff of his*. Him! My cousin squats around me, her imagined, in my bed. Her whispered breath plays through our window shook with shoulderings of wind.

Kay's tiny arms around my neck.

I hear it.

—Darling hums a deeply moo, and in her head and chest, a buzz: a scratching, stretched-on-cow-skin, record sound. Then this is all there is, here in the stall. This is all of what there is and I am in it. We are gone. We're like the scruffed and knotty boards along the stall, the hungry two-by-fours and tin in slanted scallops overhead. The devil's breath, it flits and winks in bits of fluff, and drifting dust nothings yellowed by the flashlight's filthy shine done in the shadows on the stall. I taste like teeth and morning breath and staleness in my mouth. I think of me inside the shower, Jeab, my brother, marbled clean.

The shower boys white in the shower water, beaded, tall, and fine. I stop, and zip my dampened pants. I quit it.

Just us two at night.

Us in the stall.

I sniff that spit smell on my fingers, spit and mossy smells of us. I set my bucket on the bucket stand—I milk.

And Darling kicks.

"Whoa now, girl," I say to her, and milk, my brunting shoulder on the muscle of her quarter ham to push. Darling's leg springs back to where it should. A foot of leg sinks in the mud beneath the swamping of the straw. I milk some more. I pat Darling's rump and tell her, "Good old girl. This is how to do it."

Good and warm, and all of what there is, me with my cow.

Once, she was all I ever had, back then, *in my mind*, on our farm.

Mama, Kay and Jeab, and Doll.

Jeab

Drunk? A little, Jeab says, singing this. "It's not but two
things smells like fish," he says. Jeab, tip-tap, shakes the
sack to pour the brass and copper bullets on my table with
his song. A hoarded, fistful clutch of hollow-points and rifle
.22's. Some roaming bullets curve in rolling, clean my table,
hit the floor, so glad to leave my velvet sack—these slugs,
like tiny tailless sharks, they almost grin at me and Jeab.

He might be ten here in the clutter of his sailor suit and
shells, my gun, our playtime-bright, unlikely, violent toys.
Jeab hums and figures on the loading of the pistol, nudging
slugs. We're ready, Pabst and Miller sixes, fifth of Jack and
cigarettes, the crumpled car wreck of an empty pack, a
camel crashed in cellophane, in ashtray butts and bottle-
caps, in matches, ash, and foil.

"You reckon this toy shoots through the brick?" Jeab
holds the pistol to his temple, clicks his sound-effecting
cheek.

"I'm sort of buzzed," is what I say. "Let's try to point
that somewhere else . . . You need your boy to fix a drink?
Sometimes I'm homesick for the country. I get lonely here
a bit."

"I'm sort of ornery and horny. How 'bout you?"

I'm seeing funny for a moment. What just now I've come to notice is a watch on both his wrists. "So what's all this?"

"My other watch."

"Your watch."

"Well, say this arm is gimpy."

"You'd be late, I bet," I say.

"Might kiss my life goodbye is what. It ain't for fashion tips," he says. "We aim to navigate by sixties on your wrist-watch multiplied. You know, like coordinates and such."

"Your life."

"You'd fucking best believe it. Like you'll never need to know," he says.

"Is all you do so violent?"

"We're just dogs. We're dogs with shirts on, all's we are. It's in our blood," my brother says. Jeab, loading, pours us both a Jack.

"You mean the gene pool, Jeab," I say.

"Just killing. Shallow as it is, and in the end, it's just the big ones eat the littler. How it is. You take and look back at the tree where we been shaken from," he says. "Killing. Look at Grandpa, Bub, our rotten every-mother's-son."

I ask my brother who's he kidding.

Jeab says, "True, I heard it good. Old Grandpa Lloyd—your mama's daddy—shot Pop's uncle way back then. I figure Pop was maybe one, and Mama not yet even born, Old Lloyd and Grandma not much married and no bigger then than kids."

I ask my brother when was this.

"Which rock you hiding under, son?" he says. "Old scrawny Grandpa Lloyd!" Jeab knocks a Jack back, bares his grinning. Sleeves his shoulder at his teeth. "Pop had an uncle who was screwing round with Grandma while Lloyd hunted. Well, this one time started raining, Lloyd come in too soon, they said. Lloyd caught them feathers in their britches—Daddy's Uncle Norm was hid. Lloyd blew his brains out 'neath the mattress where they did it, Mama said. One gone MF, our grandpa was. Hey, also, you could hunt the year out then and never was a limit. I bet they weren't more'n six or seventeen if all a day."

"Is that the truth? Is that some nonsense tale, you think?"

"Boy, what a sorry bunch of hicks and trash we've fallen from," he says.

"We lived okay."

"Yeah, mister, perfect."

"Well, it's true."

"The evil shit that we have done," he says. "The shit they did to us."

"What evil?"

"Tell me what of all that work and butchery was good. My God, you sick little fucking puppy. Shit and killing we had did. But now, like everything is wrong," he says. "Up next to how it was." Jeab belches. Starts in on another Pabst.

"It seems like everything is small," he says. "It seems *it all is done.*"

What we are here to do is in our second six of beers. I buzz in the Chinese man and pay for the grocery sack. We have the toylike paper boxes, sauce and gravies, soups and rice. "I miss the calm a lot," I say.

He stands my phone book on the sink.

I ask, "But hold it, what's the rest?"

"What's whaty?"

"That, that you were singing. You know. . . ."

"One of them is fish," he says. "So what all you got we can shoot at for us to have fun?"

Darling

The tidal night lies like a living thing, a sea that floods the oak trees and the fields across our farm. Still milking Darling in the darkness, I can hear our clattered kitchen's sounds of dinner through the stall, the evening whippoorwill and crickets, calling frogs tongued in the grass. I feature Mama with her pots up at the stove inside our house, our yellow, flower-papered walls all greased and blistering and peeling in our kitchen's dinner air. My mama's hair will have its ratted set, a red and also coppery, my mama in her work outfit and nylons on her legs, and at the table, Jeab and Daddy deep in fishing magazines. A bleeding chicken out to thaw. I figure this is how we are: our house an island in the moonlight. Us, our barn around my cow and me—some ship blown out to water off our island on the world.

All done, I hang my foaming bucket white with milk up on the nail. Unsnap the lead from Darling's halter ring, and let in Darling's calf. I tell him, "Get on, little dogie. Come on, get your butt up, son."

Darling's calf is like a puppy, or a small dog, more than he is like a bull. He lunges in a challengy and puppy-headed way to me, through dust swarms in the flashlight's solid shine. I can tell he's happy seeing me. He peers out lonesome dumb, caught in the dust-collecting light, and also sort of sweet-looking . . . stood in muddy pies of turd, he plays like he's a bigger bull, and shovels hooves of dirt which lift, then splash out on the dark.

Darling's calf, he scratches, looks, and tries to see if I am watching him.

I let him in to Darling.

Watch him suck.

She serves her quarters to the calf, and giving in she spreads her legs and stretches once-as-long her neck. Her chomping gnaw goes horizontal. Darling munches on her cud. Her bullock puppy of a calf butts in her bag. He bumps his nose up under her. I swear I hear some water-something dollop up in Darling. Watch the froth foam on his mouth sucked to the gallons of her bag. His milky whiskers like a cat. His bubbled lips.

I watch him, watch him as he sucks.

I turn the flashlight off on us and swallow into night. I'm blinded. Now the night grows lighter as the darkness shallows up.

—Jeab's horning voice.

Across our yard my mama's coughing bounces interrupted talk. Their tabled plates and grating chair legs sail the noisy dinner air. Their sounds rub sawn across the grass blades. Small, the bodies of their voices wade the dark about our yard.

Water. This is what there is here in the heavy wash of dark. This weirdness, him in doing her like this. The calf moans under Darling in the light slits from the windows of our house shown through the boards. His bladdered, jelly-swollen eyes wink in the skinny cracks of light. He butts his head bone in her bag like he is eating her from out of her or pulling out her blood. His mother horns at him to suckle, rests. She tongues her crumbly feed and hooves the straw and lets him suck.

Buttressed up, his legs out bracing him, the calf spreads like a tent to get the suck held in his mouth. Beside his chin, another teat is hung with milky pearls of drool. It seems he goes at her for something more than love or thirst of milk.

I don't know. Maybe it is less than what I think.

I have seen them suck a zillion times . . . I want to take his windpipe here, and choke the little fucking shit.

Out in the cooler, widening night beyond the feedlot, Darling glows. She's panting. Sand about her shimmers. Low above us clouds are waves. Are not. Are just a bunch of ices. Nightlit. Lamplight from our windows shows a lighthouse on our cow trough. Water diddles in the quiet from the hose screwed to the float. I pee and wonder where the water meets like ants run underground. Is there an ocean underground, and does the water in my belly and in the cattle want the ground? I pat the milk that's left in her. Her tuckered bones crick in her cow legs as she lolls on through the gate and to the end of our corral, where she balloons into our even brighter field out in the dark. Our cattled trail has dullish shades of things, a withered leaf of weed, a rind of sneaker, muddled shapes, my Darling glad and broadly mottled, black and white. I smack my palm across her rump. There is Daddy's truck hulked on our yard behind our house. I see that every window light is on like company inside, like Sunday, grownups cutting up with us. Or just is careless Jeab. My brother won't turn off a light. Jeab says it isn't squat to him.

· · ·

Jeab breeching free the chamber of my gun is how he is.

Jeab before. Jeab of now, and with his grin.

"So guess who milked her first?" he says. "So who was baby's best and even sweetest, special love?"

I do not remember how my brother really was.

I take my cow into the night is how I am when I'm with Darling. "Come on, girl," I say to her. "Come on, girl. Come on."

Darling plods the flowered weeds caught in the lamplight from our house that draws a glimmer on our yard and gauzes fainter to the barn like sheets of light shone underwater on our field out in the night. The muggy night works like a filter, like a scarf around the lantern-looking windows of our house. I look back, but I don't know if there is light on me or just is in my eyes. I can't tell.

Some weed runs dark half up my leg. I look at her to know if we're in light.

Darling looming in the dark.

Jeab wags the gun.

Jeab works the hammer's action back.

"So give your big, fucking brother a hug!" he says.

Look at Darling, whitely and in black done in the night!

"Come on, girl," I say to her, and I head Darling to the fence-line trees all washed up in the night.

"Come here, love," I say.

Water

I see him. Here Jeab is, a kid. Schooled in the sandlot sunlit playing field, my brother runs behind me on a warming April's day, the other gym-class boys behind us running too. I almost fall. I'm in the lead with one loose sneaker to the shower stalls in gym; the walls ahead are painted cinder-block. My air comes out a fog. Our gym coach shrills his whistled time, again. I'm nothing much but run—my brother crashing up my back. This day, most everything seems nar-rowed to the pathway to our school. A kind of line in me connects me to the gym and chilly stalls, a line that draws me like a toy across the sky between my arms, the flapping, thuddy noise of sprinters, shouting, fearful coughing me.

I cross the stairs into the shadow of the door, the empty halls. The girls all herd in through the entrance at the gym hall's other end, their flagging shirts white in the sun a moment, bunched and bobbed, balloony heads rise shaded up the stairway to the gym girls' locker room. Their girlish voices brightly tuned, a kind of song.

Chlorine and sneaker smells of feet the taste of pennies dew our air.

Into the shower, tinted windows let the light in morning

green. The clanging lockers jiggle free, the splashing guttered plop of water, laughing, faucets squealing tight.

The shower's row of rusted nozzles rain with water, fogging heat.

Jeab walks in beside me with his towel.

He starts to pee.

"Hey, Bubba, check this mother out," he says.

My brother in the shower is my memory of him. Water, hair, and strapping Jeab.

Skip it. Just forget what all of this I never even said.

Pretty Doll

See my cow that we call Darling, black and white out in
our field, out in the light of every day that is our farm. Her
grainy hide is wet in sheen of sleepy sun all over her, the
normal light across the bluegrass new and green about our
field. Her forelegs in the grass are side by side, while Darling's hocks gap in a cow step: one leg ahead and one leg
back. Darling's udders branch with vein part in the sun, part
under her, and Darling's udders glove with teat swelled toward the ever-wanting ground. There runs a saddling of
black that mottles white on Darling's side; a yoke of black
sleeks on her neck and on her narrowed head-bone wedge,
where Darling's head veils like a Moorish girl's, is black and
lower, white, and then to rubbery and pinkish where she
glumly sets her mouth.

And see how Darling holds the light in this same field
out in our world?

I watch her smallness from my window. I see Darling.
Me and Doll.

Her Heart in Her

My cousin Kay, thirteen and flirting, lets us look into her shirt front while we hoe our rows of corn. Kay leans, pretending she is innocent, and bobs across from me; she weaves and wades through the flood of green on our weedy ground. On up the field our furrowed cullises of corn begin to merge, as if the knee-high rows of corn had zipped apart about her hoeing—blending overgrown in green again ahead. And farther still, the cornfield narrows, funneling row onto row to the end of our farm, where the trees are the edge of our world. We're Kay, and Mama and Daddy, and Jeab and me, and God.

It seems to me he's left us sweaty, hoeing useless at the earth. This thistled thorn leaf spread of herb along the ground surrounds our corn, this burring beggarweed and horsetail, berried indigo and poke, the pulpy, lemon-petaled mustard, dandelion, wheaty cane.

Us in all-day sky and dirt, last year's pasture, this year's combed-in early corn. Dust. Summer's heat to come.

We're all so bored except for having her around.

Between the cornfield and the cattle field, we run the irrigation on our melons through the night, some forty automatic sprinklers. Dawn, an extra-thirsty cow will jump a fence to butt the pipes, to dash her muzzle in the water, gnaw a sprinkler's water stream.

We're in a tea bed thick of garden, sandy-bottomed, mostly weed.

Kay and Jeab hoe past on up the field. My mama and daddy, lagging, stand like scarecrows in their clothes, which rag with wind and flap their backs a dozen yards or so from me. Kay pulls her hoe out from the ground about the sucker stalks of corn. My cousin's hair falls from her neck. Beneath the skin, a string of nuts spine down her backbone in her shirt, which wraps in flannel wings around her, buttoned loosely at the front. Her hair reminds me then of boards. My brother, Jeab, with Kay, says whispered something, looks—if he were me—into her shirt where Kay is shaded, paler her hid from the sun.

Our sunburned, blond, and skinny girl.

She once let me chew her hair into my mouth like wadded silk.

Jeab does what I tried to do when I've hoed close to Kay. On other weekends with my cousin I would talk across the corn. We work on mornings when the crops will drench our thin and soggy clothes. Her dampened T-shirts sieve her skin, her bent before me cutting squash or tending laces on a shoe, her open shirt drapes in the air. We watch her seashell-colored nipples on her body while she hoes.

I mostly picture her remembered this one day, my cousin over from our grandpa's house to help us in the fields. My cousin's perfect branch of neck in yellow hair.

Sometimes her neck is like an animal alive inside of her. Inside of Kay.

Dust shuffles in my shoes and wads my toes. Here a row, here a weed, here a tug of hidey corn is buried in the dirt. A tumblebug works scritching useless circles in the dirt, little wars, its halves of back like lacquered candy on the soft of it inside, two hooded wings to shell its innards from the burning of the world. It rolls a mealy, sculpted ball of turd, a boulder twice its size behind it, reared, intent and kicking, freakish Atlas with its feet.

It wanders backwards lost and blinded toward an ant bed death to come. Me, I'm a giant to the bug. I wonder what its tiny mind is like, what nonsense it must live.

I kneel and listen at the world. I hear the gyroings and gears inside the belly of the world, oily and in tar—and in the sky, the set chain of the wider all—turns.

No. I hear out here the wind. Work. Sun on us.

My cousin's fitty laughter purls a sound up in her mouth. The rippled leaves of little corn swish on our land. A breathing wind. Against the ground the air moves down to gently nudge the leaning corn in a changing green; the undersides of leaves wave shifting shades. Crockery green and olive. Unripe lime.

I dream of her. She showed her bruise to me in school. One time alone, when I was sick, I passed the gym hall doors that opened on the gym girls' locker room. I caught a glazed and dripping girl long in a towel, a sock in hands slide up a leg. Wet on a bench, the beaded backside of my cousin in a towel, the sound of shower waters on in a steamy light.

My daddy fans his hat next to his head and scans the rows. "You all hold off and meet us up," says Daddy, slow to Kay and Jeab. They catch a glance at one another, then look bothered back at me. Kay yawns—her mouth a bitten peach. Her open mouth hangs weighed with lip the way it often, tired, will. I'm nearly crazy watching Kay! She bends and lifts inside her shirt. She backwards hoes my straggler's row of weedy field to meet us up.

"Find any corn in these here weeds?" she says.

"I lost my shoes," says Jeab. "I can't believe there's not a tractor what can't do this kind of work."

My daddy's face.

The way he stands says things to us that he does not say.

"All right. Well, I'll just do the rest," he says. "You plugs go on inside."

"Now, Joe, they're fooling," Mama says.

"It's good they got their sense of humor."

"Joe, my Lord."

My daddy plants his hoe and goes to check the sprinkler lines.

The podded weeds will live the longest, taller corn dry paper-leaved, the sandy ground turn clay and shatter. Calves will die.

A rusty nail lies bent and petrified with ruin limbs of twig, pebbles, sand in barren canyons, tinily. I'm daydream gone, lost in my head down at the small, this anted world. Some days I'm not much good at work; I'm pretty worthless, usually gone. My bug rolls through the ants stirred in a penny-colored boil.

I don't see how God could think of everything at once, each nothing twig and little desert.

I think God has turned his back on all us bugs.

When we knock off to miss the sun we are a circus in our lunch amongst the hay bales and the siloed high baskets stacked like cups out in the open, airy shed, a shed cleared empty save the hay bales, seed, and tractor in a hulk. Lunch is paper sacks: our coiny Necco Wafers, sandwiches, potato chips and Cokes, orange and grape and nut-float sodas. Nuts float in the soda neck so they're already wet each time I tilt my Coke to sip, so cold and fizzing, munchy foam.

Darling

Mama has her cigarette and figures on the basket slats some crayoned Daddy's numbers. Daddy on a basket at his sandwich seeks an outer something hazy on our farm, jawing sideways balls of lunch.

It hardly seems like God could really care.

Here are Mama and Daddy with drinks and me in tossed electric shadows of our television's glare. Kay lies on her elbows on our living-room floor. TV news. My daddy swirls the ice cubes in his glass, says, "That's it," says, "Bright-eyed and bushy-tailed," and gets up. Now it's the Late Show movie on TV.

Mama says her shoo-on-you's—her voice a kind of horn. Says, "Just a second minute. I just want to see the start. I heard about this one; it's a good picture. It was good when it was a movie, still."

Daddy swats her leg with folded news.

"Let's get to bed, woman. You're not watching no scary picture. You'll be fighting boogers all night long."

"Oh pooh. You wish."

"Let's hit it, Mom."

"I got to hug goodnight my lambs."

She hugs. Her smell gets on my head.

Kay slowly curls onto her back dressed in my mama's borrowed wrapper. Lacy roses red on pink and sleeving drawn along her legs, the trim unraveling in loose ends of its fishing-line thread. My cousin puts a finger to her teeth and bites the nail; she is a grinning blonde to Daddy while he tongues his smaller ice.

Kay is the only living girl like her around. Out here there's mostly trash and cattle, burnt-up orange trees and corn, the Yankee trailer houses scattered, colored shacks. We've got our church on up the road, a Stuckey's, Grandpa's and Grandma's tin-roofed house, the store at Cuchard's Gulf. The farms, and cattle dotting pastures. Empty fields.

A steady night-slush sound of semis on the four-lane miles away.

Some nights I'll walk off in the dark to watch the head-light's tracing beams, the faces floodlit on the billboards in the night. Driving. People in their cars I'll never know.

My daddy switches off the lamp. "You all don't make no noise," he says. "Let's keep it to a whimper." Daddy peers at our TV as if he pays no great attention to my cousin in her sprawl, her lying laid out like the wounded on our oval, banded rug.

Out past the curtains on the window brightened moon-wash frosts our lawn.

I try my bumbling look of interest in the same old picture tube.

My daddy winks at me and goes.

Mama says, "Now just this one," and then for me to go to sleep. "It's a weekend's worth of weeding, boy, before you've got your school." She says this with a face like mine the way she sometimes is, my mama's face awake and haloed and her hair teased up for bed.

I'll see my face in Mama's head.

I kiss her cool and mirrored image, leave my lip print red with wax.

"Don't be up late, you two," she says.

Mama and Daddy in the bathroom turn the bathtub water on, their voices boinging on the water. Water sploshes, muffled noise. When the water stops I hear my mama mutter something, Kay and Bub, and something other, Bub and Jeab, like everything she says to Daddy has somehow to do with me. I see their legs locked in the water and their places dark with hair, my mama straddling my daddy, then the shower. Water sounds.

Him naked, hairy in the water on my mama coupled up. I see her furred and fitting skin.

Him coupling Mama in the water as her face turns into mine, with Mama bent into the shower water, naked, me as her.

To hear their talk, my cousin fidgets with the TV volume knob. We get my mama's lifting questions, scooted seat noise from the john. I nudge my cousin where she lies down on the floor between my feet. Then Daddy follows Mama to their room and shuts the door. Their tabled bed-lamp switch is clicked. Their closet hangers softly ding. Kay shrugs her shoulders at my toes. "You best behave yourself," she says. "I'll put a hurting on your butt."

She sort of sings into these words so I will guess that she is playing: Kay is happy we're alone. I know she is. Our wooden house's hollow dark draws in to watch us in the room. We've gotten bigger in the room since they have gone. Our bodies—mine, at least, feels better-looking, rubbery, and strong. I feel like I'm not such a kid.

The light thrown from our television moves in shifting blues and grays and whitish paths of light, the dark and lighter colors shadow us. My cousin rests her head upon her elbow on the rug. She tugs her wrapper up a bit to scratch some pink into a knee; she bares her powder-whitened leg, the wrapper riding on a thigh. She smooths the fabric to her skin. Her spooning rear is woman-bigger than the rest of small-girl her. My cousin sighs a shallow yawn.

"It's getting I can't raise my head," she says.

"Yeah, girl, but don't I know."

Kay scratches, reaching at her back as if a crab is in her hand, as if a crab had left its husk and inched with fingered, meaty claws. "Feel at this knot on me," she says.

Afraid of her, I nod my head. I sit here foolish on the

sofa, sort of stiffened, mostly pose. I'm mostly bones and hands and legs. A churning curdles in my stomach, eases shuddery to calm. I get the fear and then it goes. I make a hard-on watching Kay. I put my mind inside the girl; inside of her, *inside her body*, I imagine all the colors in the hollowness of her, the tubing pipework of her blood, her netted stomach gourd in gray. The veining blue, her corded red. Branched through the organs dark in Kay, the beading cauliflower tree of clabbered, milky-yellow eggs. The stuff in her! And the hollower dark of where Kay is a girl and the wet-bag, girl guts of her. My mind lets pictures of the hair like on my brother cover Kay. I put a knob like his on her, and underneath my brother's thing, I put her lipped and pinkish hole. A slit, he says. A tongue in teeth between her legs, a mouth in fur.

Her skin pretended in my head.

I see my cousin in the shower with my brother over her.

Kay takes the television's lighting on the rug. She bends a leg across her other one, her place up in her panties, banding low about her hips. Where she has shaved, the peppered skin. She has her heart and lungs inside of her in darkness in her chest, and air is there somewhere as well, the liquid ball of light in Kay, and Jesus's face is in her, too. I stretch out my foot again, and nudge her with my toe.

This is how I picture her: my foot warm in her hair.

"You having fun?" my cousin says.

A sort of dare.

I feel a shiver shrink an inch of me; I drop my silly leg.

This is the sign from her to move. She tilts her head to show her collar's wisping, finely spun and threaded, downy blonde. She has these vacuum-hosey rings around her throat where I could hold, where I could pull her hosey throat from her—or put her in my mouth and bite it sucking from her head.

Across the television, talky, people wander on the tube.

My cousin curves into the places pressing Kay against her clothes.

I touch the nutting of her spine. I tell her, "Goll, you're knotted sore."

I'm not afraid of her, I swear.

"More near my head," my cousin says.

"Is it like here?"

"Hold at my thumb."

She shows me where.

"Rub at this muscle, Bub?" she says.

Kay stills unnormal on our floor. We are the warm that is the air; a something back and forth between us running airy, kind of hums. The air, it jitters cues from Kay to me—and back from me to her, like she knows what is doing in my head to do with her. My hard-on frog goes soft, then filled again, as I am rubbing Kay. This girl could float up like a ghost or like a puppet in the air down on our Late Show, Kay-sprawled, living-room floor.

My fingers slip into an armpit damp in stiff and twirling curls.

I get her powdered, biscuit smell. She holds my wrist against her shoulder like a hoe within her grip. She drags my hand across her skin, across the deep and heated pocket of her collar's bony ridge. Kay tinting dimly on our floor with my hand on her shoulder, says a word; she whispers almost-all-a-word, or Kay, her throat, it sort of loosens on her air breathed into her. My cousin breathes a whispered No. "That does like butter, there," she says. Inside my underwear the buzz. Here in the warm tucked in her clothes my fingers trip across the bumping of a barely risen mole. I feel the plumping where her chest has swollen ulcerous from her. Her breast is swollen as a bruise. Surprised, and not all that surprised, I'm disappointed that it's real. I feel this damp and wrinkled leaf around it, Kay, her flimsy pea.

The cooler night outside our house has settled; boards begin to tick. Out in the window stars and satellites and planets fleck the sky. There's not a soul up in the world.

"We better not," is what she says.

My cousin looks at me. We kiss.

I don't care for her a second. Well, it's true.

My cousin sits up from the floor and turns the side of her to me. She lets her clothes fall down her arm a bit, her shoulder skin a little and the sunblush on her neck. "I'll pull this off some, if you want," she says, and folds along my arm. She holds her fingers to my palm and draws me close to show me more. Her dark below her tented belly in the warm within her clothes. I see the fur.

"You like my chest enough?" she says. "You want a touch?" Kay rests her head against my legs and leans herself where we can see. Her hill of breast against her slip. Her thin and mushroom-looking nipple darkens television blue; it tints—electrically from shudders on her shadow-hued skin. Her on my mouth, her in my hand. I cup her breast as if my cousin bulbed with water in her skin. She rests her head between my legs. I feel her press herself to me, feel where the water runs cold through my hands to my sides in the cold air pipe of my shirt into me, and the shower-room cold starts to freeze where I am, where the water shrinks me in our gym.

But I am not afraid of her.

I am not afraid of her.

I am not afraid of a girl.

My brother boot-toes through the door. He's home— and my brother at our door sees my hands on the girl and the blur of my hands from her clothes. He glances leery at the girl—Jeab grins at me, his raccoon face a mask of tractor soot, and his boots in their dust give a kick at our door while my brother sees me over her. My brother sees Kay in the blue on our floor.

"It's time you got to bed," he says.

I wash and go to bed.

I hear our living-room cricks when I wake in my room, and the grunts are a girl and my brother, Jeab's, wind, and the sounds of the world are of Jeab and of Kay, when our girl on our farm in the whole wide world is the sound of my brother on her.

Another Sunday afternoon, our normal nothing weekend sunny day of sky. Outside, the weeds stressed in the wind begin to tremble, firey, in green the germing puff of dandelions, nightshade, wheaty cane. We are at our hoes in the sun where the rows seem to blend then to wedge at the fence with the trees in a line like a hedge.

Across the field my daddy yanks a lane of irrigation pipe, he straightens, walks a length of pipe, he bends again. We hoe the corn. My mama and brother and leaning Kay. This year the heat is early in on us. The burning blades of corn wilt twisted mouse tails at their ends; some weeds in bloom lose all their petals, budded yellow flecks the ground, the crickets, blackflies, ants and beetles, speckled lace-winged ladybugs.

When Daddy finishes the pipes he turns the irrigation on, the spouting fountain heads of sprinklers sputter water, pelting beads.

"You all come get a drink," he says.

We plant our hoes and come. We kneel and drink beside the water, wash our faces in the water, wet our heads. Kay goes to stand into a stream. Before the sprinkler's circled

course my cousin braces in the spray. A glassy shatter showers her. Our water darkens through her clothes and soaks
the whiteness from her hair. A pond of water fills her smile,
the push of waters denting Kay—a misted, water-headache
haze surrounds the girl. I put inside her what I see, our
house, our barns, our fields and cows. Our canteloupes and
melons wait in garden rows for rain where the sprinklers
churn.

This weevil fidgets with a flower till I crush the tiny life
of it beneath my sneakered feet.

I don't hate her all that much.

I wonder, why does God let Jeab have her . . . and not
me?

I've seen a sow eat half its farrow. All our egg yolks
break in red, all bloodshot, fertilized and veiny with our
rooster's useless seed. Unborn. We scrambled up those suck-
ers, so then, why should I be kind? I call the dustbowl-sandy
drought on us, a plague of locust, fire, on my brother down
from God.

Gunner

"Check this sucker out. We slip a nail in for a pin and sort of halfway maybe, jimmy-riggy fix it, Bubba Lou."

Across the tablecloth my brother screws the pieces of the gun, the chamber, firing pin, and hammer, bits of springs he pets like silk or tiny mice in his big hands. The dully sinking in myself in tired power from the Jack. I scoot my rice with useless chopsticks, chase the rices I can't pick.

Jeab talking just to hear his mouth. He's every Jeab he's ever been and every Jeab that I have seen.

He's him remembered on the sofa Saturdaying through cartoons; venetian blinds in streaky daylight slat the morning bright on Jeab. We sit with Cheerios and Kool-Aid in the fade of our TV. At Jetsons. Lost up in "The Flintstones," I would live in these cartoons. Another me and Jeab with magazines, a him I have as photographed: his helmet in his hands at ease, the pilot with his flight gear on the *Nimitz* out to sea. Jeab grins his teeth against the wind, and on the conning tower's industry the laundry line of blue and white and kiting, Navy flags.

Behind the glass his bleaching photograph sits framed and hinting colors back with knickknacks in our hall. Our father dead, the cattle sold. Our mother dishing still her lunches at the Stuckey's in our town.

She'll give her complimentary Dixie cup to tourists: orange drink, her bad directions down to Disney. She will warn to block the sun.

Now Jeab and I for something done while in our visit sip our beers, our bit of talk to fill the buzzing from the tube light on my sink.

Across the tablecloth my brother twists a screw into the gun. Jeab, seated, speaks to me again. He talks of moving irrigation pipe all night when he was ten, of driving long up on our tractor weeks when it would leave him dizzy just to walk the solid ground. A clash of bats about his plowing, in the moonlight, diving shapes.

He used to always be out working, him alone.

The bats like burnt and ashy pages lifting whole into the sky, the unseen threat of empty field. Frightened, boy-sized Jeab of twelve.

"We're almost here," my brother says.

"Is there one thing that you can't do?"

"I once made liquor out of jet fuel in the Arafura Sea."

"That's Vietnam?"

"That's off of Java on New Guinea, S.S. *Norman*, bored to tears."

"I heard as Russians did that, Jeab."

"You think I'm bulling you?" he says.

He did her first is what he says.

I'd hear his feet slip from our bed, then quiet. Jeab snuck through the night.

"It ain't but seldom I will lie."

Jeab bent to pinch a splinter free, adjusts the liquid silver watchwork of the trigger screws and springs. He tests the cylinder for spin; he lets the hammer's action snap.

"I bet a dollar to a doughnut we are almost home," he says.

I figure who am I to say that he is not already there?

I chew the loose skin on my wrist and smell the children's smell of bread. Suck up the duck sauce from its packet, pour more fingerfuls of Jack. I sit pretending to remember different days I've seen with Jeab. One evening, Jeab and Kay and I ran wiggly naked in the darkness in the knee-corn playing chase, their voices later in our living room, my brother and my cousin's whispered words along the floor.

I tell him, "Jarib, lean and see if you can reach me out a beer."

Jeab snags my Jack cup back from me. "Whoa, Bubba, I am getting scared. Hop off your lazy candy ass and get your sorry self a brew. You're closer. Hit it, son!" he says.

"Let's just relax."

"Come kick my ass," Jeab, grinning, says, "unless you still don't think you're big enough."

"Just asking, really. Jesus Christ. You play too much."

I reach and get me out a beer. I tap it.

I am still not big enough.

Three children pinkish in a single bath, the popping tub of water on our bodies bottle green. Our bath was hotter with the faucet on, surrounded us with tired, melty, covering our legs with squishing warm. Afterward our fingers wrinkled raisiny and dead in the clammy cold. My cousin, Kay, would wash my brother while I sucked a wetted washcloth cool with water through my teeth.

We visit talking to our drinks into the night. I think of her.

So where was he?

Bedding Down the Stall

At our dinner table's quiet what an actor I can be. Get clean and comb my hair for church. I lie, a masked and shrinking spy in the fogged-in island of our house. I hide, pretend I'm at my homework, feed the pigs. I milk our cow. I dream of Mama getting cancers from the cloud she draws in her, the slugs of mucus in her gullet, liquid cough of cigarettes. Then when she does, I feel that somehow with my thinking I have caused the growth in her. Her tumors stop. I die instead.

I draw up small into my body till I finally disappear.

I move invisible through school, at home, a shade across the table, faceless, silent save our blessing when it comes my turn to pray. Except with her. I come out whenever I want it to her, and my cow will be waiting outside in the dark with her head on the gate to our yard.

Us in the wind breathed on the darkness, ghosts, and ghostly winded trees that see the things I do with her. Trees so aware it seems that spirits stir their branches and their leaves, as if the trees were live with Indians, the Cree, the skirted Seminole, the eagle-feathered Crow. In wind, the branches dip and tremble, watch, they witness, whisper, see. A snake of trees around our pasture. Doll with me.

This night my arms are like a rabbit's arms. They're quick—I grab my bucket, go outside, and find my herd. I sneak. I draw back the gate onto Darling, snap the lead on Darling's halter ring and scratch on her back with a cob.

The winging ears beneath her ringed and thickly nailish curve of horn. I bite her ear, kiss at her head.

"Come on, girl," I say to her. The same way every time I say to Darling.

"Come on. Get all prettied up."

I lead my cow into her stall. The summer air with the smell of our farm from the hay, and our corn, and our lawn-mowered lawn, a gassy, quiet lake of air. The owling. Whip-poorwills and crickets. Television. Katydids. Our stall is cooler where the wind stirs up the hotter August dread. I fluff some hay about the stall, then tie the rope through Darling's trough where Darling noses in her feed, the polished waxwood of her trough, a woodsman's crib in a woodsman's house, a twist of cow hair snagged in wood like a furred cocoon where she has rubbed.

Some days I'll think of baby Jesus in the trough on Darling's feed, on sawdust piles of splintered grains, and husks, and fly wing bits of chaff. Chipped stones of corn and swizzled orange rinds in blackstrap molasses, and a smell—the taste of bread, and of raisins burst in bread. "Hey, get your leg up, girl," I say to her, and hear her nothing moo.

We're sleepers.

What is my memory of Darling?

Here she is.

Her evening shit as if to greet me, emptied liquidy, a splash, a plopping mason's muddy sling of her night soil. The arch of back and lifted tail, her leaking and looking back sweetly to me. Her chew of cud, the dull regard. I take the small me from inside of me to her, then I'm alive.

"Hey, kitty, get on, you old plug."

Some nights we're home too late to hope that she'll be
ladylike to milk. We'll drag home tired from a field and find
our haystack run with cattle. Mad, our longhorn in our
headlights, daring, wall-eyes coaled with murder like reflec-
tors on our road, her eating our clothes from the porch of
the morning, all of our cows in our yard lying down. I'll
come to her. I'll whack our longhorn back from Darling,
feed my sugar-pudding first. I'll milk my cow and feel the
day go dark, smell outside cool to night.

Then Darling moos.

But does she care what I will do? A giant dog, she sniffs
my arm. She needs to feel my milking her.

I watch her head lift in the window square, her horns
like devil's horns blacked on our window's square of night.
I hear the crickings in her hooves and in the air around our
world, out in the air that is the air out on this year across
our farm.

A passing cloud shape in the window is my mama watching us. The threat of her is in my head. The nosey cloud of
Mama watching gives my heart a bigger urge.

Darling does not care what kind of faker I can be. I pour
the feed. *I'm true to her.*

She turns herself before the night and Darling coughs.
She tosses snot into the fly specks in the moonlight on her
back. She settles calm. Some flies return.

I milk, and the milk rings the zinc of my bucket from
her like a pee from our room on the lawn. It sisses, like Jeab
when he leaks from our window at night, arcing crackly
and bright in the dark.

Jeab says to me, peeing, his reaches the fence.

He always does.

He's bigger . . .

God, but *she* is huge! Her stretch of chest broad as a
boat hull I could climb aboard and ride, like I could climb

up in her broadness, sleep, a bug hid in a milkweed in the cotton of her paunch.

I hang my bucket on the nail, then bring my stool around behind of her, and listen for the house.

Still not a sound.

There's not a soul out back to hear us. Mumbling Mama and Daddy and Jeab in our house in the curdling soup of their sleep. A picture of Jesus hung up in our hall and our praying hands.

I'm yawny.

Stand on my stool behind Darling. I pour water on the conch shell of her rump. I rub her off.

My pet, our bossy dappled doll. Is she so dumb? Is she a dullard? Chances are she probably is. My pumpkin. "Easy, girl," I say to her, and pat on her lovely flank. I kiss the hair that is her hide, and push my nose into the warmth that comes from up inside of her.

I say she saved my childish life. It might be so, or may be my excuse for her. It sometimes seems to me that I'm not ever who I am, without my cow. In bed or quiet in the field or on our roof up in the sun, I'll try to look into myself to see the wickedness in me. I do, but nothing's ever there. Up in the clay-lined empty well of me, not even my dry heart.

I'm gone somewhere. Some kind of monster, witch, a freak.

I hug myself hard into Darling. My own Doll.

Then the wind on our summery field comes in, in soured smells of lawn and weed, and of night on the ground, and of wood in our barn, and of straw *and of cow* on our farm.

I put myself inside of her.

. . .

Our rooster wakes me up. To daybreak. Addle-brained and achy, I am bedded next to Darling where we've fallen off to sleep. She watches, cow-content and curious while munching on her breakfast of the bedding of our hay.

I put myself inside of her. Again.

Another day.

Pilot

The closety rain on my street in the darkness outside has the world like asleep in a dream. It's midnight gone at my apartment, Jeab, my window and the rain. We have the chamber snapped in and the barrel screwed tight to the breech where it fits, and a black gum strewn on a bag, blackened 3&1 gun-oil tabletop ponds, Jeab mean in his beer. It looks like everything's under a blanket tonight— nearly everything seems to be small in the dark drawing closer around on our lives.

I'm shrinking. What do I think of Jeab?

My skin is lampshade thin and cringing, boned in birdish, girly bones, like I was wax or made of paper, how a stick will keep its shape all burnt to nothing left but ash.

I remember the hair puddled under his arms in the shower-room hutch of the stalls in our school, Jeab naked and tall in the rainwater steam, and a Jeab in our barn, our chickens, goat and horse and guineas, in my memory, three bad dogs, our needled tractor parts, and tedder, bladed harrows, rakes, our plow. I've seen our baler take a newborn calf and chug on busting wire sounds, unbothered, calm

inside. Another day a perfect bale spills with a twisted ear
or tail.

Across the table trash my brother loads our old familiar
death. "It's fixed. I *do* like live munitions! Here, get a look
at your hog leg," he says. The handlegrip sandpapers snug
in my hand like the gun wants to grow in my skin, five
pregnant chambers clean machined with the cartridged
slugs. The bullet's case. The bead of brass that caps each
charge in a comb like a wasp in its patient dark.

"Outstanding. Less see if she shoots," he says, and he
eyes down the line of my gun at me—at the phone book on
my sink—a flimsy capgun shot is snapped as if my gun were
teasing Jeab. "This piece of penny-candy shit! Aw, mother.
Jesus-fucking Christmas! Still, you flinched. You're sitting
pissing in your pants," he says.

For drama, Jeab I guess swells up to threaten me with
hate. There is this tire tube in Jeab about to blap apart with
spleen. Things want to burst in front of Jeab to save from
hanging in his air.

I sip my iced and sweating Pabst, the buzzing, fizzy taste
of sour and the sudsing in my cheek.

He winks.

"Let's try not to shoot up the house," I say.

The weight of the gun kind of sways in his hand in a
church fan melt-away wave.

I'd like to touch his freckled arm, brown, little dots.

"Relax, I really wouldn't shoot you . . . 'less there's
orders to," he says. "God, I *mind* killing. Senseless shit."

"But you're a killer, Jeab," I say.

"You fucking punk. Don't even joke with me," he says.

"I'm playing."

"I know guys would cut your throat for joking them like
that."

Jeab's freckled face is dark as planter pots of red and bleaching clay.

"This buddy—once I saw a bomber belly-flop and scratch our base. He saved his crew," my brother says. "With half his liver and his shit blown out his suit and in his hands."

Jeab gets the Millers from the freezer, sits, he blinks through all his beer.

Big sheets of metal in the sky, my brother's smoke. The pilot, Jeab.

"It's not some TV show," he says. He's still the same mean Jeab as then. Same head and hands. Jeab wears his same old faded jeans, new snake tattoo.

I get new Dixie cups for us and pour us double fulls of Jack. Find jam and peanut butter jars, the clover honey in the bear; its sticky glue tacked on the plastic in my grasp. Crackers, paper plates, we're set.

There's not a thing I have so nice as all his many-colored shells. I go to find my box of snapshots, scalloped Polaroids of us. Pulled next to Jeab I deal him pictures, show him me in Harry's Bar: me squinting, pink-eyed, at the camera in the flash. Us at a birthday party doorway crêped in ribbon, hats, and cake. Kay and our mama hanging laundry. One old, rag-ass, scraggly Hereford sniffs her dull nose at a stick held through our fence's whitened boards.

Dolly.

"Let me see them pitchers."

My new, rusted stepside pickup, on the tailgate, *Chevrolet*. A fearful dog up in the truck. My daddy's hat white in the light.

"I should've brought my naked ones. Bangers. Bangkok dollar whores dressed like a dragon eating me. Got me a sinking recon plane we snapped that over-missed the deck, the rookie pilot's still inside so's you could watch his drowning eyes. Geishas, hunnerd scrips a pop."

Jeab, Jay, and Chris done up as Cub Scouts. On their horses, rodeod.

Then it rains outside in the streetlight's stir of the pellety course of the rain in the night, and it rains as if fanned, like some rain on a stage. Or a rain in a flashlighted path in the dark.

"It could have been a dud," he says. "Hell, set us up some target." Him, his chin where the meat rounds bone is a bulb, and it pits when his mouth rumples drawn. Jeab purses his lips. He grins.

"Say, looky here," he says, and he thumbs back the hammer of my gun at me.

Jeab squinches his eyes, he blinks.

"Shit, boy," he says. "Not even my having to aim."

He aims.

A snap cracks from my gun. A popping, phosphorescent flashing, sparks. My tube light explodes on the sink. It dazzles. Light trails like a jellyfish, all starry. Now it's dark.

"You think that might be kind of loud?" I say.

"Yep. Better use a pillow. Got a silencer?" he says. "A towel. A old dishrag will do her."

"You're liable to have us both in jail," I say. "You've screwed my flicker light."

"Can't stand that goddamned hard fluorescent."

"You can sweep the shit," I say.

"She dug it. That little sow was my first."

I tell him, get serious. I say, when did he—for real?

"Who?" he says.

I ask when. Dimly, light seeps in my kitchen where my window glows to gray on the lightening dark.

"She sure liked when I was the top," he says. "Hey, I can't miss my plane and all my stuff done shipped to Peshawar. Like figure on this for luck. Them mothers. They got me my jet by the desert, some of those sand bunny chicks and not a fuck of a lot else to do, not a lot of much breathes down my neck, less a stinger or SCUD goes to stray in our air." Jeab makes a pop with his lips. "Piece of dang cake what it is," Jeab says.

The heavy of lead pressures out from my gun, while the room gathers small on the lead. In through my window slants a shadow from the window's cross of panes.

I think of a tabletop pond of his blood like the gun oil poured to my floor.

I think of my gun in our barn on our mangy old dogs and their dog heads exploding in fur. The lightning limbed into our barn. Ticking.

Mama out calling us, "What's going on?"

"You all come wash up," Mama said.

Like she knew this and everything we ever said or did.

It sounds like we said all of this long ago, that whatever has happened is happening again. That everything's already done, it seems, that my brother is already dead. The blood coming out of his ear on the floor, and the blood coming out of my gun.

I get my car extension cord lamp from the closet in the back. It makes garagey-looking lighting, barnish, swinging above on the oven from my cupboard's crooked door.

I think my drink sees what I'm thinking.

Jeab says, "I'd be snuck out back when she was just what I would need. You fuck-up. You still are my brother."

We're still who we were when we were kids.

Jeab talks like this, "I am the hostile silhouette that will not still in bogey's sights! I am the Navy winging skull come from above. I am the lightning! I am pilot. Freedom. Death."

Outside, the moon's old yellow bulb is a faded ghost in the city haze. Everything is tired from my cord lamp in the night, gunpowder pellety and tiny.

It's like I'm not much here at all. I'm like a me made in a mirror on a mirror doubling me, repeated, small me in the glass.

My waxy hand is like a mouse's hand; the clearness of my skin shows tumored arteries and bones, the branching blue beneath my skin. I tap a couple of our beers. My jar-lid ashtray fills with cigarettes and beer-can tabs and trash, his crumpled car wreck pack of cigarettes. The smoke of all these minutes lifts or ashes into tar to dust our damp and awkward night.

I see me sitting. Me. My brother. In our breathing, seated here. My brother doesn't love me much. I guess we never did.

I'll kill him.

I could kill him good.

He Hugs Us

When he is working us like this, my daddy's hat in its haloey glory, silvered ribbon on the brim like in the garden, he, our father, is this shadow over us. I'm not afraid; sometimes he loves us. He's so strong. What do I do in the shadow of Daddy out here fencing in the field? Our daddy never says a word more than how worthless we're to him. He tells us get back on our horse, to get the lead out of our britches, hoe our row, to toe the line, that he had better not see anything but elbows, backs, and asses as we bend into our field—heads swallowing deep in the flowery green—says barely more than what to tell us we're to jump for him and do.

I think he's sad when he's like this. My daddy isn't horrible or Godlike how he is. A maybe great and sworded angel. Gabriel.

We're setting fence. Along our boardless line of posts the soggy ditch beside our road; a waist-deep moat runs by the pavement. Fists of cider-colored water brew in pockets in the ditch, though on our fence rise it is mostly powdered dry. At times, some strangers in a car roar by us, motorcycles, buses, semi-tractor-trailer rigs, big whalish faces on our roadway. Gales of dirty, metal air drag at us, tear in whirled directions, madly whip as if a broom attacking, pinning bits of wind and airy static in your hair. Bored at the air the coming car sound waffles passing through my head. Some dusty moths will leave the weeds and crickets toss up from the ditch beside me pebbling in the grass. Then we're alone. We're all forgotten on the roadside of our county's grassy blur.

A downy seed drifts down our road. A stirring. All begins to settle. Nothing then.

Cattle. Shifting shades of pasture. Trees and waterway of sky. I'm holding the guideline of a wire to the creosoted posts, and Jeab is holding the post on my line.

My daddy is hatted and tamping the sand with the end of a hoe. Half here, and dithering on sleep, I think of a tree sprouting branches and leaves from the post, and I feature my planting a fence from some trees I could saw off and fence on our land. And strangers passing on our road would look with wonder where we are, at how we farmers grew a fence from planting trees along our farm.

We work on our fence in the heat after spring. We eat by the sweat of our brows and the fruit of the field, with the thistles and thorns from the burnt summer land, and the snake at our heels in the dust.

The Florida sun flattens everything down.

"Take hold the posthole diggers steady. Like you mean it," Daddy says. "Not like a sissy's holding, Jeab!"

He doesn't say this stuff to hurt us. When he acts like this, my daddy shows his way with things to us, how there's a rule-bound sort of history to doing different things, that we're to choke up on the handle, cut away from us with blades, that there are three ways you can grab a thing: the right, the wrong, and his.

He, Daddy, once was still a kid, the only son of our bent

grandpa swollen old and puffed with sun, tomato-headed, cancerous, the warts across his body spilling tiny rotting seeds. Our daddy worked for him like *he* works us, in pain and painful quiet, Daddy six, and nine, and twelve years old, a teenage driving Daddy in his lonely Thunderbird, the dashboard splashed with white magnolias. Jewel, our grandma, his first mother, we would never come to know. Drowned bathing, naked in a bathtub on the telephone with shock. They say our grandpa took to the bottle. Daddy's father beat the life from him like Daddy beats a heifer as it scrambles up the chute, or beats the hoe against a fence post, hoping one of them, the hoe or post, or maybe *he* will break.

I could be wrong about him; maybe he is hard on us, is tough, for our own good.

I'm his.

His stick-limbed sleepy kid, his dreamer, rings of jerk-off shadow mooned in blue around my eyes. The yellow glow deep in my elbow. Daddy's colt: my brother, Jeab. We should be big and better men.

He's rough on us. Sometimes he's shy.

I can't believe that he would tell us if we asked him why he is.

He might not have an answer. Buys us sodas. He's so sad. The ashy cactus where he's shaven, piney slivers of his anger keep my daddy far from us, away from Daddy's scratchy hug. He has his drink. He shaves for bed.

Dad silent nights up with his paper and his secret, muttered words. He shrugs alone, his moods, his sadness, and the violence of his eyebrows twitching knives into our air.

Daddy. Sometimes we were scared.

We're setting fence out on the day. We're in a green and shady heaven.

Here where we dig on this peninsula, the dirt gives up its colors doughy white to dun and gray, the darker cake deep in the layers crumbed with blackness underneath, water, wet comes from the earth. Where the ocean's rolled.

Our state sits diked up on the water like a causeway on the Gulf. Our coasts will flood, our glades will wander. In the rainy months of spring the freakish sinkholes often come. They make our state a soggy sponge, of limestone. Orange trees and palm. Once dry, a ditch becomes canal, so many roadside county fields turn to weedy swamp in sudden rain, a floating toilet boats a flood, a shallow yard becomes a pond, a car is sunk up to its hood in morning water in your yard. One day a sinkhole takes your house and barn and everything you've got down in the unforgiving ground.

Some dogs or chickens on the chimney of your roof arked from a pond.

Above, I hear a droning airplane hum with all its tiny lives, and birdlife—chirping ratchet sounds that mock the airplane's odder song.

Now Jeab and Daddy leave me dallying to measure out a post. I watch him fussing with my brother, me pretending movie things. I stick my arm down in a posthole, playing, making me into the picture of a one-armed, crawling man. I try, but can't drag out my arm; my rabbity fingers are stuck in the dirt. It's like the devil is holding me down, choked up, his grip held to my armpit, *him*, his hand around my fingers snug as a glove on my hand in the mud.

Big thump of Daddy's coming feet.

I see him tilted in his bigness like a walking khaki tree.

"Aw, knothead, *now* what have you lost?"

"I think his sense," my brother says.

"His sense. So you're a goddamn genius?"

"What I do?"

"Christ, fuck-almighty, boy!" he says. "What ails the

two of you sometimes?" My daddy tips his Stetson up and stares at a one-armed me. He snatches me up to my feet by the waist of my jeans and my teeth chatter nice in my head. I'm in the air—I'm all in a quiver of him being mad at me and I'm liking the shake that he does. I'll like the beatings that Daddy will give me at night in a circle around in our house.

His hug. I'll fake like I'm asleep with him, and Daddy will play along carrying me to my bedroom from our couch. I want to be lost in the crib of his arms. In his clumsiness. My dad.

But then my shoes are slammed to dirt. I'm standing, toeing about at an angle in a lean from Daddy's hand.

I have to almost grin at Jeab. At Daddy.

"Tell me what it is," he says. "Tell me whatever is wrong with you two boys. Lordy, son, say? I don't know. What is it you want now, Bub? I'm about had it."

I look to see the goofing of the strings looped in Jeab's shoes, near giggle, my daddy all lit by a fire, it seems, his anger swarmed out in the air like his hat in its halo on his head. He fans off his Stetson; he pets the brim. His head gets bigger, and then gets small. My daddy's cheeks fade a little bit paler to gray and green, cooling. Blue drifts through this air.

My brother shakes his head at me like he just disagrees.

I don't think I'm wrong about him. Daddy isn't angry half as much as worn and tired.

I think my daddy could bite my face.

I see his perfect, dicey teeth on me, a vampire at my neck. An awful angel of my daddy's face . . . that softens now to love.

A coming truck surrounds my head. Big, cindered, itching bits of smoke rain at the rushed and troubled air, as if the truck went from my stomach, like the truck could up and run me down no matter where I was. Smoke settles drifting on our ditch across the water-rusted weeds. Our yellow bus pulls in from summer school; it horns at us, is gone.

Just us and him.

I almost start to say a thing—*"My hand was in the hole. I had the devil grab my fingers with my arm all down the hole!"*

But I can't say it right.

Like always, everything I'm saying to my daddy is a lie.

He rests his hoe gunned on his shoulder.

"Bubba, what is wrong with you? Oh, William, Lordy son, you break my heart!" my daddy says to me.

This is what he says to us, to me and my brother, Jeab. "Son . . . ," he says, *"Tell me what I got to do?"*

I wish I had an answer for him then.

Now he is dead.

Blue, Blue

Once we were young.

Sunday.

Here I am at eight.

Mama's ear down near my face does like a strange and crumpled horn, turned, and pinkishly the white up in a shell, little freckles crumbled there. Paper skin. A curl of hair around her ear, around the bell. She lowers closer still to comb my hair, then touches at her tongue and blears my eyelid corner wet, my eyelid windy for a second, Mama's thumb blurred at my nose. Her powdered face swims back as her against her lipstick, red red.

"What's this bit of bug bite, honey? What's this little sore?"

She's picking. Pinches at my chigger. Pats my kneecap where I hurt, a blister; pus comes out in blood.

I watch her draw her sparking dress about the slip that she has on, so white, her body soft like ice cream at the Dairy Queen in town, cool in her fountain swirl of curves, reflected, us back in the glass.

Mom.

Mama's bureau dresser mirrors circusy with things, our

Rexall's trade: her tiny eyebrow brushes furry like to paint, and fingernail polish, jars—jelly green and bubbly and Jell-O-filled and clear—clever snapping, plastic cases plated chrome. I play this here, a lipstick thing, up, down, around, and screw the wax into its tube. I lift myself on Mama's stool as Mama monkeys with her straps, her bra and secret, powdered skin, her bathroom smell.

I've whiffed her undies in the basket, dug, and latched the bathroom door to look where nipples left their print against the padding of her bra. I thought of her.

What Mama touches at or sits on has her heat left in the air. Cotton. Now she's all on top of me around my ball of head.

She's hugging. "Who's this little handsome? Precious, you hold still a second. You don't barefoot in the pasture, Bub."

My mama in her mirror smiles at her, ahold of me, jewelry, makeup, mother, child. She pets my cowlick down and pats me gentle swattings on my butt. She'll take or leave me—queen of us. She's pretty. Mama lets me know that she's the most loved one of us. I move for room to let her sit beside me, scoot across the stool. I'll flirt for her; I'll court, or woo her with my smallness. I'm this big: my head tops even with her dresser, with my hand to make a bridge. It feels like I'm this bunch or bundle, six potatoes in a bag. This pet. A useless tiny person, me so close down to the ground, potato legs and chest and elbows, with my big potato head.

I have a closet full of toys. I have my dusty cars and army men and hand-me-downish shirts, checkers, school clothes that my mama bought on sale or swapped for stamps.

She waves her polish in the air. She paints her nails, her split and chipped-at waitress nails, a witch's hand, fingers, scrawny ring of gold with hidden letters written there,

FOREVER, 14 CT. JOE. Her hand has bluish tunneled cords I want to prick to see her blood. My mama's belly is awash with stuff in her. Well, I was there once in the dark when I was small. I had a floaty little face soft in her water in the dark, and I was sleeping cupped in her, a bean, a podded kid in Mom.

We're all done up and nice for church, my mama's dress white on her legs.

If all could stay the way it is would be enough, just me and her, me playing raygun by the bureau's makeup toys.

Jeab clumps in crashing through the bedroom on the perfect mirrored us.

"Mama, I can't find my shoe," he says.

She turns herself from me.

She breaks the warmth where we're connected, turns away from me to Jeab.

Across the floor a fade of sunshine swings the morning to her room. The slatted boards of Mama's floor are burned in window-yellow light. A dusty sunbeam filled with light shines on the boards—a lean-to, light-filled like it's something I might walk amongst and push, these tiny spaceship bits of dust. Then it gets sleepy kind of here, Jeab clubbing in. His one blue shoe and Daddy's sock dragged like a cat beneath his foot. Jeab flops machine-gunned with a groan onto her nappy spreaded bed.

We're quiet some.

He's done. What Jeab wants her to know is *he can come in here on us.*

I see she's frozen for a moment, still, and arced above me mirrored locking earrings on her ears, two silver hoops hung from her stillness, hair and head and neck and all of her not moving as I look. I see her deep within the mirror.

I don't blink, but see what looks to me like tiny *barely motions* all along my mama's long, white skin.

Her lips hide in her mouth as Mama tissues at a smile, a kiss of lipstick on the tissue, perfect her.

"You all come on before it's late," she says. "They'll hiss at us at church."

I know.

Those grandmas from our town, they'll look to see if we belong with them; they blink, then turn around.

My brother tosses on the bed and yawns a doggy, show-off yawn. He lies like crucified and fakes asleep since Jeab is dead, he says. The window's sun squared with a pattern of the lattice on his arm, his brightened arm hairs swept and wild and brown and gold across her bed.

We're everything we'll ever need right here, my brother, Jeab, and Mama and me all summer Sunday long.

I almost taste the hard perfume from Mama's hairspray in our air, and that is also all right, too, with all we have.

It withers. Now that we are happy I get mad that it will go. Will tatter, unwrap into drab the way a gift torn from its box becomes just one more stupid thing, a junking, too-loud doomajig of what I feel about our mom: this bit of *everything is good* like stuff I kick beneath my bed, which grows at night into a thing that draws my sheets slipped off of me. To see us changes how I think of us. I twist my face at Jeab. I point. "Jeab picks his nose in church," I lie, ". . . and boogers on the seats."

But I'm not bad enough to matter. I'm not big enough. I'm eight.

Mama, angry almost, snaps her purse and dances out a clatter of highheels beside her bureau—she moves looking in her mirror, quick and serious and sure of how she struts and who she is, as if her makeup-painted nails had at this minute tacked to dry. The scary shape between her legs. Her place, a faintly swelling hump that fits her dress then disappears. It's hid on her.

She's done, "Completely dressed, and all fixed up," yet pinches at her chest. My mama clatters her highheels around her bed and tugs at Jeab. She bends to secret-fold our coin for church collection in his fist.

"Don't itch that chigger," Mama says. She swats my head.

So we begin.

A shade-tree shadow flags her window.

On our telephone our party line rings weakly up the road.

Mama leads us from the sunlight in her room and out the blue hall walls on through the draped laundry junkscape of our living room, newspaper, night-damp rug, and rims of toast crusts on a chair to blaze of day outside our door, to toys and trash hot on our lawn, a whitened sky like fired nails. Out in our yard the snaggled car that is the two-tone Mama drives, half green and cream with its fine trimming, grilled and grinning, toothed in chrome. Our Chevrolet waits like it is—some other, bigger kind of toy. We crawl inside to ride on down our county road and be by God. He'll sit there bleeding in the rainbow of the windows on our church, God looking far across our churchyard up the road to watch us come.

God looking crayoned in the windows. Dizzy, I imagine Jesus in the sky across our car.

My daddy's tractor crawling grabby as a rhino at the corn.

My daddy's arm.

He waves his sleeveless, sooted arm all charred with dust up to the sun. My daddy watches us and nods.

Our farm runs back behind us, comes our neighbor's

fields and barns, our neighbor's skeletony cattle, panting pigs out in his yard, tires.

Everything is bright and flattened harshly by the sunlight.

My good shoes are hardly white enough. (The truth is, never were.)

We drive with Mama down the road.

We ride to God.

Jeab

I guess he's still a killer, bully, Jeab the older son.
   That's him.
   Whenever I see my brother, there are several Jeabs I see.
I mean, he's more than him just sitting, who he is, there in
a chair. What happens is that a memory of my brother lifts
from Jeab—*his younger face*, and all at once, a boy of six
is swimming in my vision of his head, or blurring him: much
older, present, yet also making clearer how I think he really
is.
   My brother. Something hurt him once; he breathes and
spars with me and grins. Jeab, standing, shadow-punches
once the nothing air in front of me. He sails his slow, pretended, practice boxer's jab.
   He taps me. "Easy as snatching your plug," he says.
   What do I think of Jeab?
   His Navy pants and folded shirt with collared Navy bars
of gold, these medals claim that he has worth, as if his pins
were so much money he could rip from him and trade, their
other meanings held in secret, ranks and signals, Navy code.
At times I see my brother as the Jeab who means a threat;
he ordered me, or beat me up a lot, but usually who I see

is lazing horny with his shirt off: Fine Young God. The jizzed-up muscles of his chest, the leather skin like brand-new brogans, burnished pumpkinish and tan.

It bends my mind that he's the driver of a flying Navy bomb. I can't believe that he's a pilot, can't imagine people trust him not to shatter down their throats, to raze their ships with great destruction like a dragon in his jet, armed to the teeth releasing thunder angry drunk above the world. He doesn't listen when I say he won't put fear into me now, that I won't fight. He knows I'm lying.

Nothing changes much to Jeab. He tells me, "I'll still kick your butt."

He tells me, "You're my baby brother. You're still 'bout as slight as you was then."

But now we're big. It's like we're faking we're not kids.

Sometimes moody, he'll be tired. When he's wingless out of favor, fell from grace, an earthbound Jeab—when all his kicked-back easy bluster leaves him: say our Daddy shouts at him for scratching up the truck, or skipping chores, or simply being who he is, my brother's face it sort of muddies. Puffed and slack, he's lost his edge. He pouts. His chin is down and rounder then, his fogged and fearful face is a clouded bucket of his loss where there was once a lion's jaw.

Or maybe just a someday pilot's. Small town brawler. High school king.

Does he cheer up? He usually did.

Nothing can hurt my brother.

I remember him at ten.

I see us playing at the dashboard in the sunlight on our truck. A glaze of light burns on my memory of that day, a humming, stuccoed wall of light; it moves ahead before our truck the way the moon will move with you. Heated. Damp and morning air like smoke or dew-created glare—as if a painter came along and smudged or watercolor-brushed a wash of white across the haze.

That kind of day.

Driving, Daddy with his six-pack, happy kids. In back of us our pickup truck is stacked with bales of hay, my window venting in a coolness, on the dashboard greenish pennies, pens, a chip-toothed pocket comb. The flaking metal of the dashboard seems to *age* in front of me, deep in my play. I have an army man or something in the forcefield of the glass, fine hairline cracks split in the windshield. We are small. We wear our sort of matching shirts, checkered, Jeab's in faded colors more worn out and *real* than mine.

I think that everything I have or do is play-toy next to him.

We make a pit stop at our store, at Cuchard's. Colors of the store are red and blue, jumpy: bags of penny candy, racks of orange cracker Nabs, and Squire handkerchiefs and flints, Snickers, Ronson lighters, fingernail clippers, hair barrettes and penknives, razors, railroad gloves and hammers, shovels, rows of beany canned goods, rusted sardine tins of fish, a crayoned list for pricing six-packs, sodas, bait worms by the pint, and ice cream, watches, boxes, freezer paper, fat pig's knuckles floating in a freak jar soup of brine— jarred like some oddness at a carnival, a sideshow birth from science tanked in pink formaldehyde, and guns, a bass slick on a wall plaque next to Cuchard's glass-eyed deer—this past the counter on the gun case with its head shoved through the wall. As if the deer had poked its head in just to blink and sniff hello. I dip my arm into the water of the drink box for a Coke, the bubbles tiny in the water egged on hairs all down my arm. We glug our Cokes and pay to go.

We tug the ropes and shove the bales. Jeab climbs the

stack and tells our daddy he will ride in back to watch. Towered, Jeab says he's a giant. We're all drunk in Daddy's mood, in Daddy's reckless happy knowing we will sell this load of bales. Then on we go, and in a windy little while I drift asleep into the haze, my breezy mind fine in the window. Dreaming. Things thud in my sleep. I feel a rhino in my dream bring down his horn against the truck, his thunder, hooves which rock the road and make a broomy sound of swishing like the wind wraps through the grass, then springy, grunting wire sounds, a thudding, hay bale-busting sounds. Our daddy bumps us off the road. We're shuddered. Lint and green alfalfa leaf and stems stir in the heat; a storm of dust swirls in my window, on the truck hood—twistered weeds. Behind the truck when we jump out, there is this mountain range of hay. We've lost our whole entire load. I look, but I can't find my brother. Longways stretched beside the ditch a jumbled pile like Shredded Wheat lies torn and spilled in splintered bales—as if to tempt the pastured cows our road is bedded down in hay.

Then Jeab yells for a soda from the mound. He says he's dry. He rises, falls back on a bale—a little shaken, pony-eyed, Jeab smiles, pretending from this avalanche like he has had a ball.

He says, "I wish you'd took a picture."

Jeab says, "Let's do her again."

My daddy, "You set still a minute." Panic now.

"Hey, I'm a surfer. See my fall? You catch it? Rode that sucker righteous right on down!" Jeab soaks with red bled through his shirt, a bloody cloud.

We sit and stare at our disaster.

Daddy sobs. I see my father really crying.

"God, enough!"

He tries, but might as well be cursed.

He throws his wallet from his pocket.

Daddy bends and pinches some hay and walks away on down our road.

Jeab's more than famous in our family, speaks a cowboy airline captain's calm-pretended country drawl. Jeab has a half-real Southern voice. As kids our crackertalk is drowned between Miami and the South. We have a choice. I think he chooses how he talks. I know I do. We have the television on. We figure out how we should sound to get along with where we'll live.

He never *reads* a person near as well as me. Jeab doesn't care what people think, while things like yard trash make me crazy, hate him, shame me on our bus when we are shumbled home from school. Jeab junk-connives his different forts from cast-off scatter, sheets of tin, and posts, tomato crates and hay bales, like the many-hutted pens where he has bred his gnashing dogs—his pit bulls swinging by their teeth hung from a tire swing of Jeab's. A Plymouth car hood upside down becomes our metal-flake canoe. He chains his dogs up to the car hood, has them pull him like a chariot, a king across our yard.

A hunter.

USN lieutenant, flying bomb.

Bent cruddy postcards stamped in Norfolk, Sea of Java, Vietnam.

"Um, Jeab, the neighbors here shoot back at you if you think this is play. . . ."

"I hope they do" is what he says, loading, passes me the Jack. Jeab takes a dishrag from my oven door and wraps it on the gun.

I see my brother, Jeab, at ten.

He tries to teach me how to punch him, "Son, you damn
near almost had it. In the belly, not the ribs, you idiot. I
don't feel a thing." He holds my arm so tight a headache
starts to climb up from my wrist to settle curling in my head,
his killer's hold, a hold like worms are in my arm, or baby
snakes, my rising veins. He says, "Account of your not lis-
tening to me, *here is what you get.*" He molds my fist; he
knocks my head.

I take it, hating that his thoughts are in our bedroom
air with mine. He talks at night. He jokes. He whispers.
Maybe Jeab is lonesome. I don't know.

My cousin Kay and I will hide from him or call him
names at church.

The cowboy Jeab, the killer. Something.

Nothing can hurt my brother, so he says.

He sets the barn on fire twice while smoking cigarettes
with me. He tells me all his easy evils, cups the match hot
in his palm, his magic, cupped up like a star until the flame
he lights is his. "You strike and tuck it from the wind . . .
like here." He holds my hand in his.

His secrets, shaded moldy places in the hay barn, sinful
us, with dirty magazines and BB guns, potato chips and
wine. Repentant? "Not too much," he says.

Our daddy whips him in a circle as our barn burns to
the ground, the fire sometimes leaping paper flat and high
into the dark. The flames leap twisting from the jumble,
sparking waterspouts of orange sparks which spiral to the
sky, and ashes, embered bits of wood and flaming straw in
the starry night. I watch and think of camping out. Jeab
cries and cries and never means it, blaming Daddy for the
blaze—because our father put the hay up with the dew still

on our field. It steams. An ash is all it takes to rut a lizard race of flames and the fire's swarm.

Me, Mama and Daddy, and crying Jeab.

Most every night when we are kids I feel my brother shake his bunk a soft and nudging little rock which drums me tenderly to sleep, Jeab twitching quiet in the darkness of our bedroom, jerking off.

As in the shower, strapping Jeab is sleek and stalliony and grown. He has that light within his skin, a liquid, bitter muscled oil of something burning in his arms. His arm hairs flattened in the water, wet and shimmered all across. Goliath slim in his young body, Jeab could maul or rip my lungs out, mount or eat me in the shower, tear me screaming limb from limb.

Well, we were hunters. He still is. His head a hunter's head at seven, ten, and sixteen-year-old Jeab. He saved me maybe once from drowning back when we were hiding strays, those mutts, those pups we clubbed and blasted. Me, I'd fallen in a pit, a ponded cave inside a sinkhole in the scrub behind our field. All muddy, cleft, and mossed in rock like two great haunches on the hole, great awful rabbit hutch of blackness, where it hollowed—spiderwebs. The limestone walls were green and velvet dressed with mossy weeds and shells. I tossed my dog, then slipped and fell. At first, my brother acted angry, picked me up and flicked the mud off from me, brushed my dirty head. "I reckon you're still with the world," he said.

Then knocked me down again.

Or maybe Jeab is just the way he is. His face. So much the way he was, so smirking, plucky knots of confidence, an eyebrow raised, his grin. It rarely fell, his Navy face, or changed—while mine was like a puppet's face, a stack of masks, an act.

Jeab says, *"Get me out a cold one. Sometimes I just wished that I was home."*

I asked Jeab to stay awake at night when I was scared of ghosts. He always did a little while.

What did he say?

"Oh, Bub, it's nothing. If it is—it's just a ghost, and ghosts can't hurt you. I won't let them, anyway, okay? *Now go to sleep*, already, Bub."

And he would kill whatever touched me. I was his.

My brother.

Jeab, I guess, protected me from harm.

In the Truck

The colored man who hoes our fields and cuts our melons sits his chair and bites his ice shared by the icebox out in front of Cuchard's store. He nods hello, a woman's lips, a worm of tongue that licks the ice shard like a knife is in his mouth.

"You counting cars?" my brother says to him.

"That Ford was eighty-eight. They'll be some meanness hereabouts," he says. "Your daddy's headed back."

"You reckon it? Cut me a piece of that shade," says Jeab.

"You'll need you more than that."

"I allowed it."

"You don't know for squat. Stay out of trouble, boy," he says. "Start acting right."

He licks his ice.

We plap our coins onto the counter, get our Cokes, and hit the bench. He's gone. Our colored man has left us, leaving wet spots by his chair.

My daddy pulls to Cuchard's in his primer-crusted truck, his angry head too big in the truck windshield and his hat-brim near the glass. Behind this fishbowl his hard features, mouth, his eyes that are cut from lead, his cowboy head looks sad and wrong in time, a face worn with exhausted-ness, a cowboy tired out.

My daddy all day at his work can't get caught up enough to rest. Our father works so hard at harvest nothing comes, or like the dirt—the dirt goes dry to spite us. All our calves are born in rickets. Things fall apart.

As if to puke or search the concrete, Daddy's head bends through the window of the truck across his door. He spits, yet does not raise his head again, like Daddy wants to sleep here with his face out in the air.

My brother snaps to, standing at the driver-sided door. Daddy stirs. "You boys come on, let's hit the road," he says.

We chug-a-lug and come. I slot my Coke into the bottle rack and slip past Jeab inside.

"There been some dogs back at the calves," says Daddy, Redman in his lap. He wads it, packing his tobacco for a chaw. He chews and drives, the tires scrabbling on the gravel, thocking rocks against the store.

Our truck scuds bigger on the road, then it gets small. Hello, road. We reach the trees along our land and clumps of piney oak and scrub, a wreck of rust out on the pasture, brown and crumbling, our old plow. Out in the side-view twisted mirror, Jeab is pinching his reflection, face in hands, he kneads his chin. Jeab sits the shotgun-windowed seat. I'm in between.

The singing locusts hear our truck and turn their sound down in the scrub; the country sings; our land is humming, all that engine noise of bugs. Breeding, eating up their broth-ers, buggish love. We take the clay lane by our pasture with the palm trees gone to pink. We drive on slowly from the dusk to a close-to-dark below the trees. I see a star. There is a can someone had drunk, tossed on the road and driven flat. Along the fence, along the dirt road by our farm, are walking two black dogs which turn to look at us to see if we belong, then back around. There is a third something farther, not a cow, up in the scrub. It moves the brush like it is hunting or pretending it's a pig. It crackles rutting in the brush and playing chase when Daddy stops.

Our truck rests ticking in the heat.

One dog does circles on itself, it sits. The other bobs its tongue at us.

"Let's eat," my daddy says. He gets his pistol from the glovebox, gets his gloves beneath the seat. "Those shits will run were we to shoot," he says. "Y'all call them up and pet him, catch and drop them in the back."

I see our calf is good as dead.

We cut its throat and let it tremble, watch the blood wet up the sand and puddle larger from the calf as if the blood crawled from its gullet like some red and headless worm. Unshapened, shape-shift thing of blood. With me and Jeab each holding ears, we drag the calf behind the truck. Jeab totes the calf from him like trash to not to get calf guts onto him—and Daddy kicks him for this. He says to me, will I get right and lug the calf up on the tailgate. It is now I steal some power off of Jeab, but it's too big. I have to heave my end to Jeab, and him and Daddy heft the calf on in the back. I'm weak as piss is what I think. I might as well have been a girl.

I wander, low amongst palmetto bushes, pine, and berried nightshade, thick wisteria and grape. I find the calf leg in the grass and bend its hoof how it would walk, chewed off and wet from all that gnawing. I still laugh. I shake the leg like I am scared of it at Jeab.

"It wants to getcha, Jeab," I say.

I make the leg do gentle calf walks on my palm and throw it in. My daddy spits at this disgust. He glares at me,

"Can't you act grown two seconds, son?" he says. "My Goddy! Get from me."

He pets the mangy, wagging Shepherds, rubs the gun against his jeans. "Here, puppies. Come on, motherfuckers."

Everything has Daddy worn and down, it seems to me.

We load the dogs and head on home.

Happy, dogs sniff at the calf.

We pass the shadow of our colored man, a scarecrow in the dusk. He counts us, knifing on his counting stick our number in the truck, three notches—figuring, I guess, the end and measure of our lives.

We're in the truck the same as always, this one year.

No one talks.

Leaving Town

In under the tin and the beams of the depot shade stands my grandfather watching me go, our empty bench against the station brick, before it hulls of peanuts where we sat and had our smokes. A soldier waits and folds his paper, crewcut—someone's teenage son, a sunglassed mama with her toddler, farmers, luggage carts and wagons with their crustied iron wheels, freighters, railroad tracks and engines, giant railroad tanks and trains, like toys, grown oversized and big, as if a child the size of God could come and rattle us for play. I wipe my window on the train. Inside, the same sad smells of liquor, babies, coffee spills, and must. Untethered, backward in its jerking, this old train begins to roll. Our depot drifts. I'm leaving home.

My grandfather holds out his arm up to me as the depot flows passing behind. I'm gliding, cashing in my chips, I'm cutting out, I've run away. My train rears out backwards from town in the heat like our town is what happens to leave, like our town is what happens to leave from my train sitting motionless nowhere at all, afloat; our town drifts down a river, toward the ocean, headed south.

Our dottering town and my train are aware how I think and make everything wrong that I've planned.

—My grandfather can't even see me. Nodding, he waves to a farther-down car. The Marion depot and courthouse float on with our town like a barge on a current of light. I back past the Sizzler, the Stuckey's, our sprawling mall, watching everything forward grow small with our town, all the rest of the world rolling on.

I remember him there with his arm out to me and his hat in the afternoon shade.

I watch as he fades in the air on our town. Then I am gone.

What I Do with Doll

I feel the night wind on her back as Darling munches in her feed, the lines of cow hair warmly grained against my palms—I'm on her, cock inside her darkness. In our window square of night a frost of stars above the world, all the world, all the stars, and all the light air clean around, under, on, and in between of me and Darling. There are pinwheel tiny winds on Darling's broadness spun to me, along my arms and up and down along my slaty, naked skin—wind-sweetened, swept across her coolly to my butt and down my legs and sneakered feet up on the stool, back in the muck and straw and shit behind her body, me in her. Her padded flanks slap at my knees with squishy belly-dipping slicks. There's not a soul inside our house, nor on our farm save me and Darling.

Save us, Lord.

Our night-pale house sits in the window like a whale is on our yard, aground, yet tied somehow to me. Ivory. Whalebone in the darkness is our fence across the lawn.

A panting dog fills up my chest, my mouth; my legs are frightened dog legs hopping jerkily at her. Its tongue, the red-hot of its pecker! Dog, I glance about; I listen. Are there

bigger dogs than me around? Will something kick or eat me
as I'm mounted on her hide? Everything knows I'm home
with Darling, sand and lawn and wood and sea breeze and
the seaweed-rotting straw. I've got the feeling something
watches us; the stall walls seem to breathe. Up on the roof
the loosened tin leaves from this closet in the wind, it buc-
kles: tin clunked from itself to grumble weirdly like a saw.

"Hey, *easy*, love."

She pulls away and drops me bobbing, breaks the joining
warmth of us.

Unplugging, I dry in the wind. What is it now? Who
does this mule believe she's fooling?

"Come on, Doll." I pet my love.

Her back is arched. She lifts her tail, then Darling shifts
herself to pee. Water, daddled from its parting, faucety. An
idle, glassy stream of light. I stumble splattered from my
stool. She dribbles bitter beer or vinegar in swarming flies
of smell. It steams. Her undergrounding pee like tiny rivers
in the straw as she pours liquid heat from her.

She breaks the hot and greasy magic of our bare-assed
coupling up.

Me double-fisted on my business.

Darling finishes her pee.

I must be awful, caught like this in the scary dark, me
and my cow.

I steal out milking in our barn, pretending sins. I hide the
laundry, sometimes Grandma in my mind in her remembered large brassiere. I'm bored and cruel one windy night
and feed my fingers to our bullock, let that tiny, hungry
rascal take my rod into his mouth. Delicious cracking in my
backbone as the calf sucks at my thing. It rolls its eyes and
gets me snotted, bites my skin and spits me out. Still teething,

me and it excited. Hard, I stab at his behind, but as I fumble at the calf, I hear its mom begin to moo. She sniffs at us and then I know. She has the part that I have wanted. Heated, all those dirty secrets that they kept from me are here. Such heaven, I will learn to screw! The wet and plunking knock of heartbeat as she's melting through my chest, great loaf of bread that lifts to take the skinny pole I press to her. I know that I have picked the devil, that her slot is even hotter with the hell that burns for us.

I drop my clothes and climb my stool behind our cow and I am home.

She has the sweetest part of all.

We never talk.

In our small vista of the window far-off clouds rise from the ground above the distant line of trees, long fishes, fish-gut-looking clouds which lift and roll before the stars, then lighter, backlit and divided by the Gulf-approaching moon.

I unhook my pail and pour her washing water on; I clean the pee and rub us off the same as every time with her. The night's own wind on us a warning, like a siren, winter cold.

Across the road a pair of headlights filters cones into the night—some neighbor bearded at his steering wheel and laughing as he drives through the blowing fields.

He goes to whisper to my mama what he sees with me and Doll.

We're not half-done. She thinks by peeing she has stopped me, but it just eggs on my urge.

If I look deep down into Darling—if I stare right at her hard enough—I sense while I am looking, she can almost read my mind. She shakes her head as if to ask *where is her feed?* It seems she thinks she kind of earns it since I've had my way with her. This cow is wrong.

I'm like the bull when I'm with Darling, bad and crashing with my fists against her ribs to settle her. I dump the feed into her trough and jerk her lead to play along.

"Now you set still and whoa a minute. Easy. Take it easy, plug." She kicks the boards along the wall.

Our stall—the inside of a tent around us—glowy-walled and windowed with the pinhole flecks of stars. Like penlights. Nothing matters much except for us out in the night, like when I lay across my cousin in our tent when we were nine. The bluish light on us like water, her white panties at our knees. Breathing. We were in a bubble somewhere high above the lawn. My cousin showed me what was hers. We touched her pink and fiddled mine. Two puppies tumbled in the covers with her smell warm on my arm. Alone, our family in the living room, the two of us were gone.

But now it's dark.

I stroke my cow and hold her dewlap, lay my hand against her throat and feel the irrigating heart. She thumps a life lived up in her. She maybe thinks that I'm not bull enough, can see I'm not her kind. I prop my stool and brush the fly dots from her haunch and clamber up. Aware, she kicks back where I've clambered, rocks the stool. I slap her butt. Trouble. Lightning in the stall as Darling lashes back her head the way a bass wags in the air. She bucks and swells herself to piddle, swords and scratches with her horns a shave of wood peeled from the boards; she scars the wall.

"Goddamn it!" I grab at her tail. I tell her, "You hang still, you bitch."

A toss of foam throws from her mouth. Her snapping lead attached to timber sends a shaking through the stall. I think of Kay and get all hard—I've got her. Open back the flaps of sugar's unprotected shell. Her big vagina, doo-ma-bob. My fingers slide into the grooving of the wet-mouth reach in her. When she breathes out again, I'm in.

So I'm a monster taking her!

I'm on the job.

I'm loving her.

I dip like this spills from my innards, like my thoughts of this have hardened into muscles in my arms, my skinny calves and back and shoulders, solid now, with my bad thoughts—like what I think could step apart from me, my red and meated thinking leave and leap into my cow.

A lunging hound comes from my body, from my heaving, hungry me. Then she is mine. I'm squishing fine inside of Darling.

She can't look to see the violence. She can't see where I've put in. She can't keep her mind fixed on our fight as well as me. This tired dog gives up her struggle and collapses in a tub where she is mine.

A rain of light thins on the darkness. Clouds are rags across our moon. I see the shadowed depth return to things, the wind come up and love on us as I spit onto Darling in the glimmer of the stall.

She's panting.

I'm up on her riding like my brother back of her. I'm shrinking. Now I think like Jeab.

I'm him.

I put myself inside again. I plug this awful hard I have into my pretty doll. I put myself inside of hers.

We're lovers now.

I win.

This is how we are tonight.

A star falls in our window hot and sizzling on the dark like water spat across a pan.

I love our stall! Its smell of plants green in December, how the sky turns into night.

Some darkened shape comes back to life deep in the weeds and scoots away. Things always change themselves to something else, the rabbits, fox, and possums. There are lives down in the ground, in water, mindless tumbling bugs. Mama with her pots up at our grandma's at the stove. Only Mama or my daddy ever tell us what to do. We live somewhere. We have a place here in the world where Jeab and I know we belong.

Small creatures creep along the dark and know that hid amongst the fennel they belong with us as well. The dampened grass knows us; the trees know us, and all of this is ours.

We live somewhere. We have a house here on our road.

Our morning bus takes us to school with wisping dew kicked up like smoke out on the morning, unmown lawn, and there is Darling.

Milking.

Here we ride again.

I've always known just how to work the cows. I bottle all the stragglers, runts, and baby calves and piglets with the light beamed through their ears, so thin. My daddy and my brother leave me home to tend the young. This once, I almost birth a stillborn, pull its hooves—I sit and cry.

Out near the sinkhole of our buried dogs a dropping two-year heifer, fat with calf, crawls on the marshy ground, the sawgrass bedded flat around this heifer in a cow nest. In the air, then on a sawgrass sprig, a dragonfly lands shimmering, its tail a lizard green. The air burns hummingly with insects, hid cicadas, rot and heat.

This heifer's calf has come out dead, but from this heifer only half the calf spills head out on the ground. Its forelegs, girth, and all the rest of it births unborn wet inside.

Darling

The heifer turns so as not to see me, barely moos, she huffs and crawls. This heifer crabs herself away from me, like in her head she's chosen not to let me watch her die.

As if some animals have feelings. I don't know if I can talk about the worst of what I've seen.

We winch the calf until it shatters. Tug its pieces from the cow. We put the come-along around it, tug, and break her lonesome heart. Daddy, Grandpa, Jeab, and I.

Out in the window walking cattle make a train across the dark. Sahara, caravan of cows on the quiet night. Cows single-filed out by the moonlight. On our treeline, moony palms.

My heart! She's still locked cinched against me, Darling nosing in her trough. She tongues the smaller-polished salt lick. Blocks of separated time roll on the air around the stall. We're in the bubbled separate *now* of all I have of me in her.

Like how a calf will suck your finger, I am snug inside of her. This fucking. Everything is blurred.

We're chugging, monster boy and cow.

I think of men before in Bible times, when monsters took the women and bore children out of them. The same were half-men bulls and heroes, men with horses from their muscled chests, or men with waists of fishes, legs like goat legs, feet with wings, and they were giants in the world in those old days, but now they're stars up in the dark that come alive when I'm with her. Alive in sand and straw and nail and knotted boards along the wall and in the weeds lit on our field and in the tumblebugs in corn and in the trees and in the clouds and in the shadowing glow of the night on the ground and the night-mouthed swallowing dark of our world. In things I feel alive hid in the dark about the stall.

A doggish breathing puffs from me.

I'm hollow—I can't get my mind enough off Mom.

I think of Kay. I try remembering her belly and her hair fanned on my legs. I think of gym girls in the steam, sleek creatures, thirteen-year-old tummies swelled as apricots with light. I dream of Mama in my make-believe when I see her as Darling—girls with legs held open wide to me that I pretend are Doll.

Their bodies laid out on a plate, so rosy. Skelety and budding, perfect, woman-bodied girls . . . their wishbone thighs and fleshy butts that I might break apart and eat.

A licking heat goes curling through my part, in Darling, me in her.

My Dolly shrugs to tongue her hoof. She settles tired, dull and still. A falling feather thumbs my forehead soft as down across my brow.

I gently swive myself to her is how we love. Now is how I'm loving her. We're gentle as the calves, and then the drawstring of her place sends sucking air shapes onto me. My knotted loins and silly butt and belly naked as a lumpy gourd loves close and dips to her.

We're squishing, *pip-pip*, liquid dreams.

We have a ball.

In Mama's room curled in her bureau, in their cool electric nest, her undies, spiderwebbing panty hose, and nylon wads and silk. I'd slip my feet into her stockings, stretch their sandy, rasping grip on, while my legs have gone to sleep. I'll do that. Tingling with a boner from the giddy heat in me. Sometimes her likeness in the mirror makes me think that I am Mom, yet it is just as much that I am not. I'll jerk off in her laundry, lie with Daddy's scary suit on me like *him* across her bed.

Daddy. I can screw like Dad.

Darling

. . .

Another car grows on our road; its pair of headlights gas the road air caught in funneled silt and light—a rolling roar—it passes high and then is low. Ocean sounds.

All is darker now a moment, loving Doll. Her spread of hips fit like a chairback wrapped with hide beneath my hands.

I dip and watch where we are coupled, make-believe I've crawled in her, ballooned and bowled in her large organs. In her water, lost and warm. A wormish cord up in my belly buries hot white light through me; a string of pearls pulls through my body, hot, a laughing in my butt rolls from a spool up in a hose that runs the lengthwise of my spine and to a knob where I'm abuzz.

I come. I put my seed inside of her.

I go in her unfolding, Jesus, God.

I love my cow.

Squirting. Wind turns little whispers cut by boards along our stall. I'm wrung out flat, unfolded, humming through my white and wiggly legs.

My mama's car pulls to our farm, then it is not my mama's car but someone turning in our yard back on the empty, thinning road.

A grinding munch runs in her gullet down her backbone over me.

Now sleepy, I still keep in Darling. No one's home. No one is watching. I let loose of her and feel her lose her hold on me.

There's too much wrong with this, I think. I hear the brooming scritch of straws.

Look! Look here in the shadows, something is. An upright post flits in the corner. On our hay bed, breezes stir.

As if a man swam in my vision, dim-lit timbers catch the light cool from the moon, and here he is!

The devil's legs rise underwater through the darkness of the stall, a devil's head I see imagined—I pretend he grins his teeth, a creature leathery and bearded with his bat-wings folded back. He chokes his cock between his fists and tugs it, laughing as he does. He draws his cock out three-feet-long till it is puckered in my face, a cock with wrinkles like an eyelid in my mind, a furried thing, the devil's cock-head swelling bruised and bobbing fat against my lips. Greasy. Dewdrop beads of sperm.

His thing reminds me of the colored man's. A thing furred like my brother's, or like Daddy's in the bath.

Now look again. Everything I see is in my head. I make-believe the breezing cloud with Mama's face drifts by our stall. My mama looks at me and shrieks; she will not leave.

Some monster.

I don't want to think how many times I've had our cow. It hurts to know I'll pole our cow again! I bite my stinking fingers. I go out into the pasture in the night to talk to God.

Darling leaks.

Some nights Darling leaks herself on me.

Outside in our boxing-ring corral, I dip my frog off in the trough water, splash the water lappy on my legs and on my belly. Threads of wet where we were coupled shine and run off in the moonlight, other stretchy stuff from her between my fingers and my thumb. My sneakered feet are packed with sand, manure-clumped on the flooded earth. I'm at the bottom of the sea. I wade a seabed of regret on my old iron-weighted feet.

Up in my head I think the words that come from me to speak to God. I think the words that he would want for me to say. I make a place inside my head, a hollow drainage pipe of space where I can go to talk to God.

I think the honest way I sound when I'm alone. I make my normal, quiet voice—the me I hear when I am vacuuming or happy in the tub. I hear his words. His words are serious, and higher-skulled and larger now, than mine, a wooden sound like my old grandpa's. Tired, echo-filled with loneliness or coffeed, morning calm.

Now God is speaking through the pot or covered dish that is my head. This is what he says.

I close my eyes and hear his words.

"SON," he says, "WHAT DO I GOT TO DO?"

I have this room inside my head, a lightless, nightmare kind of room that I pretend is where I am. A smaller me sits in its darkness.

Mama's car grows on our road; it blathers. Daddy's mumbled talk and bumping car noise walks our lawn.

I start with "Lord," and then some fakey words that don't sound right or *me* enough, a crippled link of words that sound like me when I will lie.

My thinking fogs. I drift, forgetting what it is that I was thinking as I prayed. My family, Mama, Jeab, and Daddy shove and crowd about my brain like mice or bugs inside of me, like beetles. Everything I'm hearing here, these layered shelves of voices, God and Jesus, Kay and Mama, Jeab and Daddy, comes from me. It's almost all that I can do to use the normal voice I use. This ache of coiling, springy fear surrounds my throat up to my tongue, is rusted, chalk dust on my stomach. *They're all home!* My dad and mom.

I see my girls spread naked wide again, my cousin with

her slip up to her waist down on our rug. I taste her hair.

My mama's head stares at us horrified across our clouded sky. I get very still. Then for a minute all of this seems like a dream.

This part of it is true. I'm finished. I won't come to Darling.

I am done with this . . . I'm through!

Bent in the lamplight sits my mama with the curlers in her hair, our shoeboxed fuel receipts and seed bills and the bank crate on the floor. My mama pencils at our table near our Mason creamer jars, the strainer sieve set with its filter and the wooden butter skeel. Our kitchen walls around me yellow, dinner smells. I am a flower-swallowed bee. We're country people in America at night. Our laughing TV chatters loudly through the kitchen; speakers bark.

I check my pants for dirt and hairs. I strain our bucket full of milk.

My mama coughs. My mama doesn't ask what all I've done while they've been gone.

I take my bath and go to bed, burrowed, drool wet on my pillow with my cover drawn to me, but as I tighten down the sheet enough, as I seal off the darkness, I am safe from every evil that may crouch about the gloom, unless my feet stick from the sheet, or if a creature finds my hand that falls with sleep before the floor. Then I am theirs.

I tug my pole. I let my breath fill up the cave I make of covers on my head. I peek out cautious on the air.

Against the ceiling I pretend to see this locket face of Mom, like she was something that the dark wore in a photograph of her, the locket Dad has of my mother. He would tell her. She was his. He'd tell her everything I did.

Darling

My mama floating near the ceiling stares and waits for me to speak. *"Oh, Jesus, what do I got to do with you two boys?"* my mama says.

She's home. Where I have picked the devil. Home.

I stroke myself to hell.

My Place

By now I've half decided how it is we're going to die, Jeab
gone to elsewhere in his liquor, me—I've wallowed on the
thought that I'll be shot down like a dog, or struck with
bricks fell from a window, held and throttled while some
killer smacks a hammer through my skull in a squirt of pain.

I drink. I touch the baby softness of the spot between
my eyes. So tender, I can see it happen, see my milky, silver
ghost seep from me, rise up through my alley and these
tenemented lives, lift from the natter, shed the city, spread
in diesel wash, dissolve.

Who knows? So many times I've felt that I will get it in
the head. This notion hits me like a memory, a string around
my finger for the things I've yet to do.

Jeab, muddled, passes me the gun. Jeab veering with
drunken but delicate steps careens and stumbles on his duffel
in my cord lamp's shifting light. Shadows—shifting shadow
men are flickered giant on my walls.

Jeab, lit and wobbled as a wino while he nods about to
fall, totters, stops as if to pose, a nodding drunk and druggy
Jeab. Before the chipped bone of the porcelain, he lines his
target objects on the soapwell of the sink: my single egg,

three dented beer cans, and his leopard-dotted shells. Jeab seems to sneak up on my sink as if these things might see his coming and, to mock him, run away.

Laughing, grinny cups and knives, a birdish scissors by my dishrack wants to chatter things at Jeab. It speaks, *"My God, but you're an asshole! You can't see enough to drink."*

Jeab loops the dishrag on my pistol. Sits. He looks for me to shoot.

"You're kidding. Jeab, you can't be real."

"We're playing. Who is there to hear?" he says.

"A billion Puerto Ricans. Jews and coloreds, too, I guess."

"You figure?"

"God, you drunken shit. We can't be shooting up the house," I say.

"No, see, that's why the rag . . . it makes my silencer," he says.

"Hey, Jeab."

"No, serious," he says. He folds my hand around the barrel on a bandaging of rag. "I mean like they won't hear a *peep*." I see him headless as a dummy in the cord light, guillotined. Jeab sweats down his temples drops of liquorated beads.

He's nutters. Jeab tilts like the blow-up clown that we would punch as kids. Big blow-up bull's-eye of a nose. Those colors! Gumball red and yellow, super blue like in cartoons—our baby, Kay and me would play with it in dirt beneath the porch. We hid. We dressed our cats and piglets while the dog would watch and blink. I sat on her. On top of Kay. I squashed our blow-up clown and Barbies, hugging, squatting out her dolls like they were calves between her legs, birthing, bottling out from her stomach like the babies of our love. I kissed her then.

Jeab, leering, tries to joke around with me and mimics

how I frown; he frowns, he wipes his sweaty forehead slicking sweat back in his hair, thick shoebrush hair that lies and bristles, rising lawnish from his head.

I can't keep a smile on me. I can't make right my face. It jitters. Nervous crawling moodiness with strings that tug my cheek.

He's fallen. We're here in the world. Outside, a clatting jog of footsteps rings the concrete on my street, a scrape of tires at the streetlight. Down my alley, motors drawl.

City. Rainy in the streetlight, clouds of heat in the paling dark.

Jeab stacks up a castle of the cans across my sink.

I thumb my gun and watch it talk. It snickers. Weirdly, I can see a living grin is on my gun, the sneery lip curled in the trigger and the pistol's hammered brow. Clean metal. *Hey, there, Mr. Shit. Hi, killer. How about we fool a little? How's about some fun?* It wants to spit its ball of flame at Jeab. Its blood soaks through the bandage of our silencery towel, pours from the barrel to the table, floods the black and crappy checkerboard of tiles across my floor. Great puddled Jell-O flood of blood. Then it is gone.

I'm sick. My throat goads up with swill. A poison mushroom cloud of headache swelters red into my brain, bursts into storm about my temples. Tiny lightning bolts of pain sear at the nerves behind my eyes in a blinking blur.

I'm where you are when coming down from all the liquor that you've had. Gas colors bloom before my eyelids, blind in hurting. Flowers swirl. I drink to chase what I just drank, hung over—drink to feed the pig in me, disgusting in my orneriness, and hungry, dumb with beer. I drink to keep myself from seeing who it is I've come to be.

My brother. Jeab picks at his rear and proudly nods at what he's done.

I hold my pistol to his liver, nudge. I put a hole in Jeab and see him squealing on the floor!

We're here. The beer and many seashells set my table like a meal.

Jeab feels my pistol press his rear.

"No, really. You're first turn to shoot," he says.

"Don't say anything to Kay about the cow," I say to Jeab.

"You rascals. You all come wash up!" Mama says.

I go to her where he has been.

I pull her lovely folds apart and put myself in hers.

So Jeab goes riding on the cattle. Quiet, Jeab sneaks out alone with her, his feet up on a bucket or my stool hid in the night, like he's a bat sucked to the cattle. Pulling, stealing heat from Darling—she must feel the heat from Jeab.

He pets her.

Gets up on her body, draws the lead in through her halter ring, and ties her to the trough. His clumsy hand rubs at her dewlap as he calms our feeding cow, her broadness black and white like fabric. Patterned, musked, and warmly odored on her scratchy, cowboy hide. Like I do, pumping away at the girl. Out in the window, stars and satellites and planets on the sky. He drops his drawers around his feet the way a child will do to pee, to watch it, cock cool in the winter like he holds a wetted thumb to chart the humming of the wind.

He takes her, *takes his stupid touch to her*, his dirt where we were perfect, Jeab and Darling, me and her.

His smiling teeth bright in the moonlight. Jeab, my brother, makes her his.

. . .

"You're fucking useless, Jeab," I say. "You're blotto."

"I'm not drunk, I'm drinking," he says.

He knows I'll give him slack like this, too gone, and not accountable enough for me to judge. When he has sat I stand my phonebook on the counter by the sink, his leopard seashell on a Miller; next to this I set my egg, which rolls in circles on itself, alive with chick, it wobbles, rests.

Bullies. One dog burst an eyeball while I shot at it and laughed. Another lashed out at my brother, gnashing spotty-mouthed for Jeab.

I sit and wonder on the ricochet of countertop and wall. I guess the distance that a .22 will whistle through my wall, counter, sheetrock, brick and mortar, then the air, buildings, baby in its cradle with a bullet through its head, a rod of light poked like a laser from the bullet through my wall in a winking hole.

My wrapped-up gun looks like a popgun with its rag hung like a flag.

My brother mutters in his beer. "You reckon Daddy ever has?"

"What's that?"

"With heifers. You know. Jig?"

"My God, get off that nasty trash. I swear, you really take the cake."

"Aw, Bubba, you'd fuck almost anything with legs if it would moo."

"Lord, Jeab, you really take the cake," I say.

"A rat if you could catch it. I would, too."

Inside, there crawls a sour wad of pissed-off, clever snakes in me. This bloat goes up my stomach through my neck into my head where the headache tolls. I'm full of insects stinging nerves. Vomit, spit climbs up my gullet. I can taste his queasy cigarette with every breath I take. I smell me breathing where he breathed and chase it back with Jack and Miller. Metal fuses to my fingers where my hand heats up the gun. The patient pistol's threats of violence climb my arm into my brain, in brass, in tin-roofed pain and thunder.

Fuck him. "Why don't you get hoof-and-mouth and crawl somewhere to rot." I'm aiming, "Boom, boom, boom," I say.

He's fading. Now I'm king of Jeab.

Killer.

I fist out my pistol at the stack of cans and blast. A target can snaps in the air and beer drops glitter from the drinkhole, spinning. Noise bumps from my ceiling as if furniture is moved. I shoot a smudge into my counter. Chalky ceiling powder falls like in a magic show on Jeab, then dusty, sulfur smells of gunshot, violence, plaster, smoke, and burn. It's like the lead squirts from my thinking, from our anger, scarily.

I'm so excited by my luck, I throw down, aiming at his shells.

Explosion. Wall erupts with egg.

"Hey, really. Now it's my go, Bub."

I jerk the pistol up from Jeab.

"Forget it."

Jeab tells me to share. He whispers, "Give her here a minute. Listen . . . easy does it, son."

I tell him, "You don't get a turn."

"Hey, give it. Give me here," he says.

But I don't care how much he's bigger. Baby. Sad and sotted clownish, Jeab can hardly keep his feet. Cross-armed and leaning with his rear against his chair back by the light, his blinky head bobs now and then, and when he turns to see me aim he almost slips from where he's settled, knocks the cord which rocks my cord lamp, casting dimness on my room, like spiders; agitating shadows grow to large and teeter smallish on our kitchen's cluttered stage.

I'd like to pistol-whip my brother with his fairy dust of pollen from the ceiling on his hair. He'd strip. I'd hold him with my pistol, spread him eagle on the floor.

There's orange yolk spilled up the wall, across the countertop and floor a honeyed oil slick of beer, my shot-up tube-lamp glass in fragments, snowy film brushed on the glass chips white as china on my tiles. I wish I cared. I blow his polka-dotted seashell into bug shapes in the beer.

"You're not so tough," I say to Jeab. "You go to hell."

So where is *he* when I am sleeping?

Where is Jeab while I lie down and dream my perfect, empty farm, no houses, nothing left but cattle and the mountained, yellow hay?

Jeab pokes at her. Naked. Clothes around his ankles. Tall, and milk blue in the darkness with the moonlight on our stall.

Does he slip in his curvy sausage through the hole below her tail? Press at and split her slitted pudding, shove it? Wet there with his spitting and her pee dripped down their legs. Her place, the beard like on a Chinaman, the silky wisping hairs like on the pizzle of a dog.

So where is Jeab?

So what is *he* so busy doing while I dress myself for school? Feeding? Working with his weights? Or packing *Jeab* back in her carcass like a duck we stuff with gruel. Does Jeab touch Kay and fuck with her? My brother's sweat greased on her knees as Jeab and Kay lock in her furring, girl and boar mucked in the living room, her butt rubbed on the floor, and after, does he tell her laughing how he saw me on our cow?

Or is he buggering our bullock? Has his cock blow down its throat while I pretend that I am sick to stay alone at home with her. I pick my breakfast-oily eggs. I con my folks. I think of Doll.

I wish for black and white, her withers, udder, fetlock, ears, and horns. I dream of Darling with the cattle in the pasture grass—does Jeab?

I love her more.

So where is he?

Then why in hell does Jeab have her to put his dirt and touch where we were perfect, where I was?

She says to come out to the living room when Jeab has gone to sleep.

Kay takes my hand out from my covers. After Jeab.

I point the barrel at my brother. "See this? Get down on the floor and say you suck," I'd like to say.

It rains. The rain with the tiny hands it has is clapping in applause.

Laughy. Raining little eyes.

Our Father

Before the blinding white of church a row of tombstones lines the graveyard, shaded, pine-straw-wreathed memorials and wild bouquets from farmers for the dead outside our town. Such gardens. Gravestones hewn of cinderblock, a shrine made like a doghouse with a plastic phone for Jesus as he makes his final call; rough, faceless, mossy cards of slate without a flower, without name. These markers bob in green wisteria beneath the weighted oaks, great limbs of vine which run the graveyard, crawl the plots, and hold the stones. A sandy car lot crowds our church, a lawn, the walkway to the porchstep. Siding. PENTECOSTAL HOLINESS in plastic on the sign. *Know that the wage of sin is death*, it says, then high above the doors the tinted windows of our church where Jesus stares. He lives in there. Pale passing clouds wad by the window with its shovel shape of glass, its colors blacked out by the shadows, him inside.

Our muffler crumps across the quiet, stirring moths up from the lot.

High on the tower's cross of iron rests a bird pitched in the wind.

We park. It sees us. Caws. It flies.

Darling

. . .

Fanning, neighbors wave their hats and printed church fans in the pews. I'm backwards, counting all the creatures in the glass above the doors, angels, Jesus and the lambs. A crusty nest hides near the ceiling wrapped in wires, rafters bare. The attic air tells of an unused room, is stale, dry like a hammer, chalk or aspirin, cracker, tin. My mama tugs against my ear to settle down and sit around. As if a parrot pecks my ear—her hand and candy of her fingers, Mama snatches me around to face the front and sing along. She's bothered. How can she expect for me to turn from him to her?

She's mad.

I turn myself for Mom.

Our lopey preacher clears his throat, goes to the podium, and speaks. We're called on. Neighbors shuffle standing like they do when we're in school. I take my Bible, *Christian Youth*, the little blue one Jeab and I scratch off the crosses marked on front to get the foil beneath our thumbnails with its rich and holy gold. My head's too big on me in church. The heated, mothball-smelling air, perfume, the oiled and vinyled woodwork rolls an ether cloth of restlessness and fidgets on my head—while Jesus staring at me feels as if a bug is in my hair.

I'm good. I sit here like my brother. I bet Mama doesn't care, but I'm aware of how she thinks church ladies watch the way we act. They're fatties, pink and green and yellow boxy dresses, flowered-on.

Kay, Grandpa Lloyd, and Grandma Delphie have the aisle on Mama's side, my grandpa pulling at the pew before him. Tiredly, it seems, he leans and keeps this empty bench from rising straight up off the floor, old swollen man and blue-haired lady. Dreamers. Mama's face and mine in

Grandma's wrinkle-laddered skin. Retired elderlies, and teens, farmers, farmers' wives, our choir, and some twenty fitful children row the pews ahead of us, singing, parting through the pages, people shifting with their weight as if to brace themselves for blows or standing zombied at a job. A paper crayon-mangled Mary and an inky Sunday program litters heel-marked on the floor. My cousin Kay dressed up in yellow almost glows like she's a ghost child in this dimly windowed hall. She acts a lady, well behaved, her hair up splashing in a bow.

God in her hair. I know he's there. He's in the heat against these walls trapped like the air capped in a jar, or like a firefly or hornet with its head pipped at the glass. I once caught smoke fogged in a jar to save for later in the day.

It faded. I forgot to watch.

I have to peek and see the glass where things are staring back at me, apostles painted in the window, one man petting at a lamb, this other man before him praying like a Jesus on TV.

Whispers.

Mama bends to Jeab and finds his *Gospel Book of Hymns*. She stands him right in a singing pose; she bends to me. I read the words. I work my mouth like I am singing. Since I'm small I get to sit if I am tired on a pew, braced by the grab of my bare legs to keep from sliding down the seat. My feet hang stuck out in the air. Our pew refuses quite to situate my small-fry seated butt. With store-glass doors and chairs and water fountains, small fry doesn't count. Nor toilet holes. It seems that everything's sized in *giant*, like their bed big as a boat on nights when I climb sneaking in. I'll make those noises of the mattress wood, their crimping springs and sheets. My mama wakes and sends me back before my daddy wakes and does, but it is other nights when Daddy wakes and says to get on in. He tells me, "Get up with your daddy. Come on. Get up here with us."

So I would crawl in with my father. Long and wooly blanket legs of his would stick against my skin. His breath. His stained and sour odor like a cloud about their bed, liquor, cigarettes, and powder, Mama's perfumed web of hair, my daddy's arm logged on my stomach to her body curled to me. Small like a goldfish, palmed between them, warm and snug between their sleep.

I fidget lint balls in my pocket. Pick the crust up from my kneecap where my chigger wants to scab.

—If I were quick to whip around, if I could peek back at them fast enough, I think I'd see them blink or catch the blood bead from his crown, in glitters, dripping down the glass. I can't remember how to follow what it is that we're to sing. I'm lost. I'm crushed beneath this holler, noise, and nonsense, stiff. I'm dead.

I might be wrong about him, maybe he is nothing but some colors painted there: his tears a streaky mark of tea stained on the cartoon of his head. Behind me, Jesus in the air.

Our preacher leads us in the song, so low and baritone he croaks while roaming reached out with his hands as if about to snatch a bug. Our choir sings. My mama widens with her eyes and meets our choir in the song, loudly. Singing fills our church from choirboys and flowered girls, their voices joined as little winds all in a storming rush of song. Our church's ladies pipe a noise. I feel my bones buzz in my head. I see my skull and all the bones in rotted clothes beside our church: dried paper faces in the graveyard flaked and dark down in the ground, their crooked crosses leaning mossy, gristled fingers deep in vine.

Our preacher calls above the song. It scares me sitting

here to think that he will call for me and Jeab, his wobbling words weeped to the ceiling as he calls for us to come.

My cousin, Kay, looks back to see me, grins; her tongue pinks out to sing.

"Confess your sins before the Lord," he says. He speaks, I guess, to me. I knee back all the way around.

Between the faces on our neighbors in the jigsaw-shattered puzzle of the colored panes of glass, all leaded, stoppered up with caulk like on our bathroom's broken tiles—*I see him bleeding in the window.* I catch Jesus as he breathes! The pane with Jesus in the window rayed with window lights of sun, orange, green-leaved with the tree leaves. Sky. A blood-dark beard and mustache with those thistles on his head, a robe, the white lamb by him petrified that wants to lick his hand.

I'd go. But I'm too scared to talk and not know any of the words.

"Bub, you sit right," my mama says. She slaps my leg.

Our preacher, testifying, hollers for the crowd to come to him. He says a sinner yearns for truth, his mercy's love, today, in church.

I kick my mom.

I'm too afraid to go on up.

My Sunday shoes have too much scuffing on them.

Somewhere home the devil waits to find me in my bed. I'll call for Dad, but not enough to wake my mama in the dark. I'll make my nightmare call to Daddy, crawl on up and get with him. I'll dream of whales and raining frogs and scary tales told in the Bible. I might run outside with Kay. It seems like everyone is waiting for a storm to shake this room, a limb of lightning through the window, come an earthquake, frogs, a plague.

Two farmer kids sift through the middle of the aisles and go to him, a girl and brother-looking other, she in gingham, he in jeans. I know them. I pretend they're me. I see me kneeling with our preacher while the blood runs from his fists, me kneeling full of shame to Jesus, too afraid.

I hit at Mom.

My mama asks what is it wrong. She mumbles, bending near and blowing puffs of whisper in my ear, a wordy lizard in my ear that glides my throat inside of me. Up close she tells me not to squirm. "What is it, sugarplum?" she says, and tries to pull me next to her.

"Hush now," she says. "Hush, little bug."

"You hurt my chigger sore," I say.

I turn away from her to see. I turn away from her to Jesus, hatefully.

Now Jesus lifts off from the window like a cloud face in my mind. I see him smudged up in the air high in the light above the crowd, a cloud of Jesus twice as large as sometimes billboards on our road, him hanging raftered in the air, him watching down. He's in our church and cars and houses and my bedroom on our farm, with Daddy hot up on the tractor. I see Jesus like his picture, on my mouth, my back, my hand. His plated face deep in my shoulder. I see Jesus like the ghost that slips like smoke inside our walls, a Jesus flat beneath my mattress mad with night noise in the air, shelved with our knickknack family photos, kids and babies, Navy cousins, married young, our older dead.

I'm good.

No, I'm not very good, or even *brave enough*. I lie.

"Almighty God," our preacher calls. He shifts these kids before him, standing, his big hatchet-fitting hands set on their heads combed to a sheen. He says to throw away the works of darkness and put on the armor of light, that in the last days when he will come again to judge the living and the dead, the holy Ghost, one God, now and forever.

We amen.

Now Jesus lingers from the window on the high walls
of our church.

His painted face floats down to mine.

I think he frowns.

Kay flutters down our church aisle in and out around the
gauntlet of our church's taller crowd, yellow there and there
and slapping with her hand to count the pews. Kay makes
a bounce outside the doorway to the light and waves *Come
on*. I hurry, too, and pass through khaki pants and shirts of
farmers, mouthed scowling, squint-eyed on their jawy wet
cigars. A farmer boot-toes at some gum clay, scraping pink
across the steps. We run outside into the sunlight in the
bug-whirred summer air, to white outside and steamy lawn
heat and the blinding, sandy lot. Sky almost everywhere
you look and even sky along the ground, the white church
siding throbby white, and lower, flower-bedded roses, kum-
quat, gladiolas, phlox. So perfect, pink and dotted violet,
greens and yellows set and eager as the icing on a cake. Our
church has icy whitened walls. A rusting padlock on the
doorknob bleeds its rust red down the door. Now Kay and
I run for our Chevrolet, and hold each other's hand.

We both run laughing, same as love.

Above our car, a weavy canopy of oak leaves makes a
shade-tree jungle hideout for us. High up in the tower live
our preacher witch and Jeab. I duck with Kay below our
bumper. Mama and Grandpa and Grandma come on outside
while Jeab peeks out behind them.

Our old Chevrolet will hide us.

The smell of love is in Kay's shining hair.

White-yellow, hair-colored.

. . .

Darling

Mama and Jeab and I drive down our road, my grandpa and grandma and Kay behind us in Grandpa's rusted melon truck. I nid-nod almost napping with my head against the door.

Our black-eyed house is sleepy home. My daddy, hatless, sits on our front-porch glider with his jug of lemon tea. His feet in socks heel on our funny papers. Everything is fine.

No, nearly everything is wrong. My daddy isn't pleased that he's the only one at home; he doesn't like when we're at service Sunday meeting in our church.

A doorless fridge lies in our yard.

Out in the pasture grass our puppy tries to mount our neighbor's sow.

"What's good for lunch?" my daddy shouts. "Who's helping Daddy drive the tractor first to cultivate the corn? Where has Daddy's cubs run off? Hey, Bubba, listen. Son?"

Inside our house I close my eyes and lurk, a blind man in his love, my arms waved baby-fashion out to scratch our blue hall walls and somewhere bump before the framing of our bathroom's open door, our knickknack pictures on the bookshelf with our family looking on. Our bathroom air grows cold and nearer to me. Somewhere closer yet, I sense the ghost that haunts our hall float with its claws out for my head. I'm blind, and scrunching up my eyes, I feel our sink's fat bar of metal mapping other things along. It makes a map of where I'm standing. I think sink and comb and makeup and these other things in here—these things as pictures in my mind while I go feeling for the soap.

I run the bathroom water on and wash my hands and shut it off. I touch the bathroom mirror's flat and sticking glass. I turn the knob. Now Jesus's blood runs from the faucet on my hands made in the dark.

I cup my palms and drink from him.

Then hear her come.

My mama asks me what I'm doing here, her hand up at her hair to snap an earring from her ear. She fans a yawn, and saunters slow into the blue about her room, the daylight white outside her window. Mama hums.

"Come on, let's see that leg," she says, her powder in the air, cool in our hallway, Mama's song.

I see him breathing in the mirror, *me*, with Jesus on my face, again. On me, the painted him. I turn and take myself to Mom. I turn and lead my way to Mama blind and reaching for the light. I come to Mama, Mama's awful, lying son.

She pulls my shoes off and my socks, then wings her arms behind her back, unhooking clumsily her bra.

We sit undressing in her bedroom, us, like we are all there is.

I sit with Mom.

The Turn

Our father's arm.

I don't remember what we've done. He goes alone into their room to let his anger stain the air.

We are in our bedroom. We are waiting to be dead.

A kind of trail to where he waits for us, a monster movie's stalking to his room is in my head. Jitters. I can feel my stomach load the nausea on my throat, the bitter, cheesed and clumping up in me: a bird on wire legs. Already I am tired from the whipping he will give. Already ache as if I wanted him, can feel his heated hand on me, can feel the strings of fire in my arm held in his hand.

So first we hear the heavy shoes. Their boxy scruffing on the floorboard, zipping slither of his belt, the tinkling bell sound of the buckle with its tiny clappered pin. I guess I'll say how weird the air is, how it gets throughout our house, though mostly back in our small bedroom and the blue walls of the hall. His sound comes rumbling and solid, groaning, rolling for our bedroom like some marbles on the floor, our tired father blown with anger, gagged with madness, gone insane. Like lead or iron leaves the paint and fills our mouths and stains the air, electric, sour as a battery you suck between your teeth.

He beats us.

First I hear my brother.

Then my daddy comes for me. He takes me just the way I've wanted, holds my hand just like a dancer, leads me, walks me through our circle like we always used to do. He sometimes sits to catch his breath, then starts to turn with me again.

Dancer. Me in Daddy's hold.

That part is hard.

Yet it is *easy* next to hearing what our father does to Jeab, and *easy still* next to the showers when in gym we'll drop our trousers with the strap marks down our legs.

He loves us.

Watercolored purple on our bodies from his love.

Now the Dark

Inside my mind big on my pillow filled with trees and sticks
and cattle like a pudding in my brain, I dream I'm floating
on a corner of our dark and curving world. Well, there's
the sky, stars, and planets on the night out in the dark. I'm
in the air. Up there I dream and think I feel this with my
body in my mind above our far and tiny farm. Unwound,
I'm flying drowned in dream light by a clear cord, water,
hope, half a birdless narrow mile from my dark bed, and
Kay is up here, too, somewhere. Our house tilts toyed below
me by this cord looped through the air. Our bead of porch
light makes a railroad model, sponged with crusty trees
beside the matchbox on our yard, our house, our chicken
shed, and silo and the crawling plastic soldiers of our cattle
by the barn.

I know so many twirly things that I have felt or ever
done. I know I'm dreaming, too, asleep. I trust my head. A
yolk of boneless yellow egg, or oyster. I'm in every dream
that I have dreamed of, flying me.

The rings of Saturn, moon and clouding. In the crowded
deep of night I see the strobe go by me flying on a many-
windowed plane.

I get this backwards, nonsense falling feeling down, this heady blur, like I am balanced on a fountain's crest of water in the air, some woody cork or puff of milkweed, like a kite—that's how I am. A kind of light strings from my belly, shining, birthy string of light. My body draws out high and corded, floating free out on the world, like it is hope that slows my falling, bird: I think I'm in control. Then I am falling by my lack of hope; I'm roaring toward the ground.

This means I'm dreaming faith in me, I guess. A moth caught in my rib cage circles batting at my heart. Not so much falling, but the world rushed up to smack me with its ground, its bready dirt, our grassy pasture, then my cord reels me back falling into small and sweaty sleep.

I'm not really Christian anymore.

Now it is dark on my bed. There are these stale and sour armpit smells of sweat on me in bed with lifting colors from my living heat, and itching in the covers, heat of overripened crops, of rotting canteloupe or squash, of failure willed, of floating failed. I can't even live right in my sleep. I'm dead. I'm useless bedded here.

I still have to live.

A twisted, stubborn fold of cover ropes like fetters on my legs. I fluff my cover spreaded big. I'm still not good.

I have these half-remembered other dreams—a patchy bunch of nothings somewhere soon before my floating, weird old things. A panting dog across our yard, the murdered colored man, a war. I have these turning television-channel memories of things: me in a movie-lobby limbo waiting ticketless, alone. There is this hot one afternoon when I am small, when Dad and I have dragged my bed out and are sleeping on our yard. I take my orange plastic rake and rake and scrape at Daddy's arm. There are these sun-cured swarms of air on me and Daddy in the shade. I guess I know that Daddy loves me. We are shy. He holds me shyly in his arms. His arms have smallish stalks of hair with bits of light like on a fly wing blue as iron on his hair, each tiny cell reflecting light—I want to shrink myself that size, and walk, a small-as-nothing farmer on the garden of his arm. These dreams remind me of some other things, and other times with Daddy. Or these things get me to think of all these things just as they are.

I wake to everything gone wrong. There's too much hoeing in our corn not done. There's too much work at home and stuff at school I have to do.

We try, but rot eats up our farm.

Another winter night, awake, the blue milk moonlight all outside has folded pane shapes through the tall and frosted window to my bed. The windowpane runs out its shadow like a crossroads on my cover: there's our church and Cuchard's store small on this snowscape on my bed, a car, the tractors in the pasture, tinied cows and tiny lives, and both these plane shapes gloom like they're alive, like ghost light shades my covers. In the night air, stars and satellites and planets on the sky. Around our world, half light and dark, there burns tomorrow's awful day. Beneath my bed somewhere is China, hell is deep beneath my sheets.

I'm *never* getting out of bed to ride our bus to school.

I'm never getting up for work to hoe the corn with Jeab again.

Feel my brother's breath squirm like a worm out from his head, turn down his mattress on the bunkbed, spill and spread in wet disease of him still breathing, in our room. My brother, Jeab, is just as solid as Play-Doh modeled man, a clod asleep, and in his belly all his guts are fished with bone.

Flat on my back, I watch the faces float in darkness in my room, fat, fuzzy, turning wads of shape—these figures blend against the normal, shift, then swirl up into spirits in my curtains, clothes and bookshelves, and my scary, headless chair.

I'm not alone.

I ease my covers off and think of Kay and do the dirty rest, my bottom bunkbed rocking quiet, Jeab the giant, dumb above. My mama and daddy dream their crops and sex and dollars past the hall. Our faithful animals outside slog in the grass blade by our yard. I fist my spit against my hard-on, feel the ghosts that haunt our hall bob with their faces in my room. These ghosts are not my dreams of ghosts. These ghosts are real. They have ideas. I sense the face of my dead grandma rear her cold and shapened hatefulness like horns out on the air.

I try to keep my mind on Kay.

If I could only turn a light on, make a noise and wake up Jeab. I'm not the only thing alive that thinks and breathes, awake tonight. *There's something more.* A something more and else is watching in my room wooled in the walls, racked in the stuffing and the slats behind the sheetrock of our walls, a something more than is my brother, bedded, breathing out his sleep. A something living, human, is . . . beside my bed.

I see this woman in my room.

She's here!

She stands by my white body, so much realer than my chair. I think she's Mama by my bed, but when I reach out to the dark, I see she's not—I'm dead like her.

My mind, my eyes strung to my thinking send a thousand

crouching spiders of my fear loose in my skin. Great sacks of fright lie on me weighted, fear like many jangled wires twists with acid through my veins.

I'm ice. I watch her in my room. I see her slip is blue, her hair is blue, her arms are gray as razorblades, her face is dull as lead. This woman moves her grayish hand to touch the grayness of her chin. Her see-through slip with its drab lacing shows her nippled, stony chest, and in this slip her woman's body and the dustball skin of her. She turns to listen for the door, and as if walking into shadow or through smoke clouds on the ground, this woman ghosts into the dark, mists through our hall, she disappears.

I call. I yammer to my brother, stutter soundlessly for Jeab.

Some nights in blurred and bothered dreaming in the closet of my sleep, I dream I fight with Jeab and win, but without strength, without his trying. I am chased or would be chasing, rocks and sand and marshy water or some chain would hobble me. My clumsy gun would only sputter. Dogs and yellow, green-eyed lions and the colored man with ice. Or I am falling from some window or a crumbled, loamy cliff with snags of grass tucked in my hands, or being stabbed or stabbing back, in blood, in bare, abandoned houses, walls with stained and shedding paper, glass and chair legs trash the floors. Or I am wild out with my cattle. Grazer. Naked as an Indian on Darling in the stall. And some nights, maybe even flying, not with fear, without my doubting. I am flying without wings. Below me, I can see the dollhouse of our barn before the cows, our yard, my brother in his sleep, but when I wake there's nothing there. I lay aware of just these shadows, shift, then wait to dream again.

.   .   .

Then Kay is here.

One night I wake into the dark and see my cousin by my bed. "Hey, come on out into the living room," my cousin's whisper says.

Her whispered breath puffs in our air. "Come on, and hurry, Bub," she says.

I close my eyes and pull my covers up and try to fake asleep, like with my father when he lifts me, when he picks me up and carries me, his possum, from our car. He holds me knowing I'm awake, so limp; I'll play asleep to ride. I'm happy then. He holds me light.

God, I'm not pretending this at all. She takes my knob.

Kay runs her hand beneath my covers in a cold and roaming tunnel through the snow across my bed. Kay brings my thing up in my covers.

Us. Then everything is changed. I fly with Kay. I know at last I have some proof that even ghosts are maybe real.

If all these things could be with me at night then why not me and Doll?

Outside my room our bluish ghost wades through the moonlight on the night.

I Sit Here

I sit and tap two dimes together, hitting one against the other.
Making sounds.
It sounds like this.
Tapping.
Dit. Dit. Dit, dit, dit.

Often I am sitting at my window where I live, a heat, or shaded, water coolness of the day against the glass, or lying nowhere on my sofa, senseless, random in the pictures on the static of my sleep. I'll see this me inside my head, this other picture of a time—thirteen and scary with a pickup, while I'm always some odd feet away and *looking at myself* like someone else remembering me, an orange soda by my mouth, a bike, our camouflagey birches peeled with bark beside our house, but it is never all of every breath of just one afternoon: one time . . . my arm out in the light, without much clarity or sound, without the rest of the rest of my life around it. Days are clouded out. To moments. I don't know if, truly, I remember right at all.

The Way My Brother Was

So we are here.

Outside my window we are mirrored sitting smaller in our chairs. I'm like my brother in the distance, us, a head-on pair of puppets trapped and dimly past the glass, an us a hand could wrap its fingers on out smaller in the dark, out on this stage of our reflection with our bodies in the air. Us floating, yellow-faced and jealous, broken little window dolls.

"Get down on the floor and say you never did," I say.

I'll break him.

We're still in the world, the blocky shadow of my cord lamp shifting shadow bars and continents and mountains on the wall.

My brother sits just as my memory has him, addled at his sea things on my table gamed with shells, doodly, toying up like army men his trilobite and seahorse, mussels, marbling on the gewgaws of his sandbox sandy shells, a hornish, spiral coning cowrie flecked with cocoa, scalloped shells, mollusks, abalone, limpet, and the flaky chambered nautilus—a screwed and snailing curlicue whose crosscut through its housing bares the spinning inner heart, hollow, anxious as a hurricane, like Jeab dumb in his drunk with all his life inside of him.

He's still a boy.

Brother. Jeab is shy and tender. Jeab is scared of me, I think. A poor and rained-on, flimsy porchstep of his eyebrow clouds his head.

Me, I'm miraged out in my window with my loaded Mr. Shit. I see me swaying in the glass. A smaller, dark and evil me—pretended, rain-streaked in my window—waves and rams the loaded pistol down my brother's gummy throat, explodes a bullet through his gullet, snaps a copper ball of fire out his butt into the floor. This window me jabs at his mouth and blasts the teeth pink out of Jeab, and shoots a burnt and bloodied puncture like a pencil through his eyes. A dreadful Bub looks back and threatens me to live as big as Jeab. I'm goners, bullyish and ricocheting anger from my brain.

I hate him. We're here in the world. It leaves me ugly with disgust that he does everything I do. He has to eat, he drinks, he empties. Creature. Jeab like me, wants pleasure, needs the touching of his skin.

Some pet, a pup or nudging dog, Jeab paws his horned and leggy spider shell and offers me his smile. I see that Jeab needs me to love or maybe me to admire him. I'm boss of Jeab like I've been kinged. Deep in the window I am fingering his every single move, my puppet, drunk and mumbly Jeab. Each nothing shrug and fussing movement that he makes, he makes for me. My brother checks if I would like what all he does before he moves, as if another tiny me up in his mind were running Jeab.

It's true. I read the ways he hesitates. I make each breath he breathes.

Jeab slips a pinky in the drinkhole of his wrinkled can of beer.

"You'd fuck a pig," I say to Jeab.

"I'd fuck a sow and it had kittens."

In my mind I make my brother lift the can stuck on his hand. I feel the can around his finger, biting. All I have to do is *not to watch*, to worry Jeab—I know how to work him. I can make my brother hurt.

"God, make me come!" my pistol cries. "I want it." Swollen as a garden hose, my mean and greasy pistol, like a cock, begins to twitch. It trembles wanting for my brother, beating throbbingly for Jeab. I guess he thinks I might be careless, miss, release the riggy trigger, spilling accident in here. He's right. I'm not all that together. I might try again with Jeab. We used to fight when we were kids.

Jeab as a child would knee my shoulders flat and pin me on the grass, Jeab with his hammer at my teeth, the nutty pinch taste of the hammer wood, the handle in my lips, the pointed yard grass sawing antish in my back.

I wrote me this—I scrawled a closet baseboard message to my life, to later me.

I cried and ran into our bedroom in the quiet of our house. I knelt among the rubber faces of our toys down on the floor. *Jeab beat me up*, I crayoned there, *never forget*.

I never did. His prickly slap, his hit, my toys—I bit their cheeking rubber faces making chewed-on dolls of Jeab. I made a promise in my closet I would fight with him and win. I must have killed him, oh, a billion times, but I was always his, and long as he would do the work for us they loved my brother, Jeab.

"Did you know Daddy used to joke about your weights," I say to Jeab. "It's true."

A juice as if from peaches wet his chest big in the sun,

sweating, Jeab pumped up and eager, Jeab would toss his bending weights to let his thunder shake the ground.

"You're fooling."

"Lord, you drunken shit, you'll miss your plane if you don't leave. Hey, where's your cigarettes?" I say. I feel a pocket of his coat, but it's his tie rolled in a ball, and in another are his crumpled cigarettes, his fliptop lighter with the winged medallion Navy fighter skulls, this silver pin roped with an anchor of the Navy on the world, four bands of yellow on his coat sleeve. On the counter, big white hat.

"Yeah, Daddy laughed behind your back how you were always so intense and into all the shit you'd do. You know, when we were all worn out; we'd call it quits when it was night, hoeing, finishing the plowing. Daddy'd let you do our chores. He'd tell me, 'Jeab's so big on muscles and his brownie points with me, I think we'll give the lad a present. Let him wrap this sucker up.' He did. And you'd be out to midnight. You were flat out born to work. I mean it. Lord, but you would go, and we'd fall over almost, Jeab. I tell you, we'd near laugh to die."

Jeab driving nights up on the tractor as he chased its sweeping light. Jeab driving nights up on the tractor, weeks when it would leave him dizzy just to walk the solid ground.

My brother.

Something hurt him once; he took his loss out on our farm, and it was Jeab alone at plowing where he found his place to be. Jeab went somewhere. He had a place there in the world with things where Jeab knew he belonged.

Pistol. Seashells and a helmet in the dragon of his plane. So where was Jeab? Then where was Jeab when I was sleeping or I dressed myself for school?

"We called you 'Cub Scout,' Jeab," I say.

"You're lying."

"Nope, I swear it's true."

"No, really."

"Honest, Jeab," I say.

Of course I say this just to hurt him. What was true was even worse. Our daddy never let my brother have what Mama gave to me.

"No, don't be shitting me," he says.

Like in our booth back in the diner. Crying, maybe Jeab was five. The other eaters in the room would pick and glance at mewing Jeab, my mama red and peering sideways like to steal a piece of fruit. We waited. Daddy gone insane. My brother's doughy little hands curled into small before his eyes. In secret, arms beneath the table, Daddy snaking off his belt to swat and threaten death at Jeab.

And later—broke my brother's shoulder while the smoke rose from our barn.

He beat him. Laid into his hide like Daddy walloping a sack against the blaze that crawled our yard, like whipping cattle with the bullwhip, aiming, carpenter, it seemed, or farmer scything down the cane.

My daddy laid into my brother like a dancer swinging Jeab.

My daddy's arms. My brother Jeab had burned our barn down.

Well, we are so alone. We walk our lives out on the farm.

We hide.

We go into each other. Jeab and I fix us a place where we can play when Daddy calls. My brother takes me with his cigarettes to show me how this time. We hide off climbing to the hayloft, matches, magazines, and wine. We cave a hideout in our hay barn, dig a tunnel in the hay bales nearly four-boys-wide around like we are down inside a well, the hay bales giving off a steam from summer rain and barny heat, from rotting water in the bellies of the bales all through the fall.

Jeab makes to show me how to smoke. He lights his cigarette while watching me, his showing somehow easing me from feeling this is wrong. So we are thin, conniving kids. Deep in the mountain weight of hay—a huge and shaggy, living monster thing we crawl inside to hide—we drink and bloat up on his cigarettes. My brother with instructions while we poke his magazines.

We sin. I race my whacking brother.

He, his thing like in the shower with the hair around his knob. The glassy roddings from the faucet, sounds of water on the tiles. Rainy.

We have only us hid in our lives back in the barn. We smoke and watch how fast our cigarettes will light a straw of hay. We stomp the flames and dare each other how much loose our fires get, the heavy tonnage blocking sounds and hiding secret wine and smoke. The smoke twirls bluish, lifting faster from the straw and genies up, dustdevil swirls of bluish smoke in tiny irritated storms.

Jeab reaches nigh above his head and lights a bale like just for fun.

I watch the hay go bright with flame.

I see our trunk of hideout air green into heat, and sulfur white, a ghostly smoke—then fireball, our hideout's steamy bales above us squirting flames and chasing me. The air above us rolls a great-balled fire cloud, an orange boil, a fire light above us first . . . then there is nothing but the smoke.

Jeab yanks me head-out by my hair. I'm baby me hauled in his arms. Jeab drags me head-out through our tunnel in the smoke like in a dream. The winter noon outside is brownly everyday. Jeab says to run go get some water and my bucket from the house, the fire folding to our barn roof lifting tin, and hurrying—as if the fire over hay knows where to move and wants to reach, as if each flame has it a hunger or a spirit in the flames. Behind me whistling cricks of fire sound, what else around is still.

Such wide and keen, impatient heat! These flames all twist and leap the hay as if a toothy yellow fire spout were sucked into the clouds, and ashes, embered bits and fireflies whip sparking through the night, in a starry yawn.

We watch it, stand out till the dawning when the window glass in diamonds flecks the morning hills of ash. Soft little smokes yet from the ground, like in the distance on a hillside tiny army fires lie, the blackened bark charred off our cattle stumped and cooked out in their soot, footless.

Back up on our porch my daddy grins beside the door. He waves his flapping happy Stetson and a feed sack at the land, my daddy's mouth a drawstrung hole to blow some birthday candles out. He waves his shirtless, clubbing arms before our barnyard up to God. My daddy coughs at us and falls. Our father.

Christmas on our farm, my brother Jeab has burned our barn down.

Then everything is wrong. I feel that hope has left our farm. Our very air falls with the ashes from our cattle on our lawn. It seems that every jot we have—our powdered car, our house, our yard, each object dusty as a playhouse, dully rusts itself to soot. As if our world were breaking up, this ash does not come from the fire but is flaking off like paint from nearly all of what is ours.

Dissolving, everything is lost.

I think if hope is not around, then where, *if anywhere,*

is hope? Then where is Jeab while I am sleeping? Where is he?

I share his beer.

We break his one last filtered cigarette to finish up the pack, me snapping one-hand with the lighter, lighting Jeab as well as me, then slip his fliptop in my pocket.

What I am is not as strong as all these things that we have done, and not as strong as what will happen, or as awful as the evil I have started here to do.

His many seashells set my table, cluttered, not so much a meal as something seed or bone or bread crust we have crumbed off from our plates. I take his beer can in my hand and mold an auto crusher's disc. I herd it flattened to the others on my table like a coin.

Life like we are is every day that I have ever lived with Jeab. In him, my memories of my brother. All his faces in him layered on our old and younger days. Jeab in our bedroom beating off or in our shower stalls with me.

I kill his stained and grainy cigarette. I spit, and suck a couple of the bullets in my mouth, the tart of copper from a bullet head slid out between my lips.

"It's just you're jealous, son," he says.

"Hey, Cub Scout. How about a shine?" I tell him no one trusted Jeab. I say that Daddy always laughed behind his back when we were kids. "He used to let you do the work 'cause you were foolish, Jeab," I say. "He used to beat you. Mama too, but never me, and anyhow, if you remember, brother, who burned down our barn? So, who was milking her?" I say.

"So who was first?"

My brother Jeab.

As long as he would walk our farm there was the memory

like a picture of our burning barn on him. A kind of drawing
of our barn, as if a funny-paper cloud were scrawled that
always followed after Jeab no matter where he went, working, lifting with his weights, or at our TV on our floor in
its faded light. My daddy never gave him slack. And when
he did, then I'd remind him what my brother was, remind
Dad of the awfulness that Jeab had done to us. He ruined
us.

I hated Jeab. But even then my brother loved me.

I was small when he was big.

Jeab gentles out his square of shirt and Navy pants from in
his duffel, draws an iron from his briefcase like a corded
metal toy. Jeab starts to iron in the dawn and steams the
heat slid on his shirt sleeve pressed across his smoking legs.

We're finished.

"You weren't even big enough to do her, Bub!" he says.
"I used to pump her shit for breakfast back when you
weren't big as this." Jeab's thumb and finger tell how big.

He doesn't hear me give an answer. Jeab has cut and
done with us. He's flattened, wooden as a signalman. Jeab
snaps his flagging uniform and dresses up for death.

His naked chest upwedged and bellowed with the swollen heart in Jeab!

Killer. He would have these strings, a leash, a net of his
protection that connected me to him, thin red umbrella of
my brother. Like a puppet, I was his. He should have left
me in the fire or the sinkhole mud for dead.

My brother. Jeab, I guess, protected me from harm.

We shoot our strays.

We pop them petlike in our feed barn with their thoughts

still on their minds. Smiley, panting, brown-eyed dogs.

She hollers. "Stop with all that racket. Y'all come wash!" my mama says.

We drag our sacks of dog across the pine straw on the ground, on ivy vines and weeds and briared all around us in the woods, on bracken baskets there and elsewhere, leafy green and ribbing fern, with pads of deermoss on the straw—a copper green like little railroad model trees along our trail—on down the holeward sloping ground and through the spider-netted leaves to end at two white peeling dogwoods near a clearing and the sun.

We drag our sacks out on the grass around the pond hid in the woods.

We find the clearing tall in pond grass rimmed with spindly yellow trees. A dragonfly darts at the air; it flutters, helicopter bug that hovers guarding on the pond. It shudders blurring toward us, dips, then disappears. There sits a rainbow-shattered other on a sprig; it flicks its wings. It chews its pencil-scribbled legs.

Along the grass high on the edge around the shoreline of the pond, my brother cats some careful steps and swings his sack while peering down. "Come take a look," my brother says. The sinkhole pond down in the hole has sucked away into the world, and in the mud down where the pond was yawns a black and jagged hole, a caveman hole which drains the water, den, a place in where a bear, a troll, or something like a zombie or the devil might would hide, his oily gyroings and gears down in the bottom of the world. We drag up, fearful of the sinkhole, through a rotten wall of stink. The place is waiting for us there. A sudden buzzing of cicadas, heat, and ticked within the cattails misted gnats lift from the hole.

As if the place knew who we were. It knows us, knows the secret things that Jeab and I have hid in us, as if the hole remembers everything that we are here to do. We live somewhere. We have a place there in the world where Jeab and I know we belong.

"We'll have to land them down its mouth, our only chance," my brother says.

Jeab swings his sack around his body, heaves his dog into the daylight, sends it hanging in the air.

Kerplosh, it makes that water sound.

Across the shattered crockery of this dry and cratered pond, I lightly toe out with my weight. I'm skating, swinging with my dog the way my daddy does a kid, the ground all breathing from the pit, it seems, the water in the sinkhole from the waters on our farm. Our water runs down under Florida. A sea is under us which meets the oceans and the Gulf, in the gulping world.

I swing to throw my sack of dog, but then the world begins to move. I fall—regret like in a car wreck—calm, the world walls out around me backwards falling for the ground. I see some trees rush on the sky, their mosses bending in the breeze. I fall like dropping toward a swimming pool. The hard and shining pureness of each thing is sure with light: but slowly, pines and pond and pebbles, tires, waxy needled sawgrass, cut-up Clorox bottles, teeth. I fall through air on me like rain, a fall like spinning underwater and my body in a ball, no weight, like I am made of cotton with the air big in my chest. Crashing. Red and numbing colors strike and mud slides at my back as if with anger, slapping me—my rib cage breaking like a plate—I hit the bottom wet and sleepily exploding things in me.

I sit and die a little while. I kind of like how I am broken; this is home. I hope that I will never leave, lost in the pit like something swallowed, wasp or moth caught in a throat. Down in the stomach of the sinkhole. I see faces in the darkness, frightful faces of a nightmare slung in mud across the walls. The oily colored man and Grandma, other things that I have known.

My brother leans out in the sky above the sinkhole mouth to see, blueness, fairy-dusted freckles on his arm in little dots. A fluttered darning-needle shimmer settles sideways on his head. "Don't lift a hair," my brother says.

Water, dimness clears. I see, beside me, swollen up with rotting, sits a maggot-matted possum leering greedily at me.

"Don't even think of getting up," says Jeab, and reaches me his hand.

My tiny life held by my brother with his bigger life in him!

I feel me squashed across his Shepherd, then I puke into the darkness, in the water. I am gone.

Jeab, I guess, protected me from harm.

But there is nothing in the sinkhole, mud, the possum, dogs, and guano in the hard, a taste of cardboard, stale and sour, deadened air.

I thought our ghosts were waiting there. I make-believe that they are there. I make the devil up like God has done— who shaped that horny head the way that I have done with God. In a reddish clay. I make a clay doll, wadded man and throw it hard against our barn.

I think that God is in the sinkhole with the devil, watching us, but I am God. I am him. I am all there ever was.

Jeab swings me stinking from the sinkhole in the woods. He knocks me down.

I wish that Jeab would carry me again.

I'd kiss his head. My brother.

This is how he is.

. . .

I set the paper cups for us and pour two fingerfuls of Jack, one cup unsettles by the splash just at my pour, then settles back. I spit a bullet like a grape seed in the cup I make my hand, load Mr. Shit, and spin the wheel. "You weirdness. What if you had caught some barn disease?" is what I say. "You should have never messed with her! I loved her, Jeab."

But he was bigger next to me. I had no hair like on my brother's. Kay had seen. She touched me there. She ran her hand beneath my covers through the snow across my bed. Kay sat her body all around me like a mouth came out of Kay, and where I poked was like a tongue, a tongue, a part come from my stomach I could loll inside of her. I pushed my pole up into hers. I put my seed inside of Kay.

So why did she let Jeab have her and put his filthy touch where we were perfect, where we loved?

Those days in gym before we shower, how I run! I hide in gym. I cross the stairs and through the shadeway of the doors and empty hall, the girls all herding in the entrance at the gym hall's other end, their flagging shirts white with the light, and shining, wild and childlike mobs of girls go bobbing up the stairs into their locker rooms to change. I try to get me wet and dressed before the older boys can see, but now they're naked in the water, bathing, boys already splashing in the shower-water fog, my heartbeat awful as a chicken's heart, and all of what is skin on me turns blue and into small, turns hardened, stippled as a chicken's skin and drawn up into plum, and all my blood is shrunken, too. A fever. Everyone in school will know what Jeab already knew. I draw my gym shorts off and tightly cinch my towel around my waist. I do my clothing neatly rolled. I do my socks undone and roll them in my locker in a ball. I putter clothing on my bench until the older boys are dry. They doddle, sparring with their voices coarse and sawing on the air—their words are rust, then boards, then tools: machinery, iron plates and chains in things they bang about the room, as if the sounds that leave their mouths tell what the boys had wished they were—I'm less than trash thrown by the road, just nothing, me and all the others with our bald and scrawny knobs.

Some of the younger grades with me sit waiting girlish in our towels, or strutting, addle-eyed and fearful, white and pearly-butted girls, while tall and animal the older boys are sleek in wetted hair, fine, dark and flat on their wet bodies. In the water, shifting hairs.

I crabwalk sideways with my back turned at the boys and find my stall—I see mine tiny as a bean, a seed, the innards of a chicken Mama slings out to the dogs, while theirs are muscled up and turkey-necked and brown and forked with veins. We smaller boys amount to piddle, salad. We aren't even girls.

This all the morning of the second day of seventh grade in school.

So Kay would know. Kay, Mama, Jeab, and even Daddy. Everyone, and all the world.

The older boys play in the shower, heated. Steam pulls from their bodies like that smoke is in their skin. Like Jeab. A frost wet on the windows. Hanging, scaly drops of water weave in beadwork down the walls. As if the tiles turned into water, or the group of things like water, plastic, Jell-O, oil, or ice, and from the nozzles, watered roar. Chlorine and feet the taste of pennies, dew the clouded shower air, and here is Jeab. He grins again. He puckers and blows me his kisses as I soap my slipping feet.

A lean and fifteen-year-old Jeab steps in the shower-flooded stalls, the glassy shower water shattered off his chest, his flattened hairs, the waters bleeding on his belly down his legs, then into steam. A wash of vapor glazes Jeab, a heated fog of whitish cloud. A rising steam cloud clabbers wet on Jeab, evaporated milk. The washing boys about like horses in the rain. One chocolate dark and others tan and pink and greasy white ones splashing.

Jeab walks in beside me with his towel. He starts to pee.

"Hey, Bubba, check this mother out," he says. "Hey, look it this big sucker! See it? On your knees!" he says. My brother in the water turns to show himself to me. Jeab bares his teeth up to the shower nozzles's glassy water rods. Jeab, beaded, shines; he rubs his throat; Jeab strokes the muscles of his chest. Upwedged, and wetted, fine, and bellowed like a swollen heart in him! My brother naked in the shower water shakes himself at me.

I try, but I can't look away. I turn and show my own to Jeab.

I show myself. I let him see.

Jeab big as life inside my kitchen in his Navy coat and drawers! Where he could mount me like our bullock or his dog down on my floor, or with his hammer at my lips down on the grass out in our yard. Jeab big as life inside my head, like Daddy is. My brother's arms! I make the blood pour on my table from the barrel of my gun.

I sweep his seashells to my floor.

Outside my window, past the mirrored us, the night has lightened still where nothing moves, where nothing lives outside my window on the ending of this night, puppets, maybe mirrored us, but nothing real. Jeab grins, a soldier with his duffel, like a movie star of Jeab. The bluer, early morning dark has paled my streetlight's milky green. The rain has stopped, the night is windless. Sleeping, everything is still.

"Well, sweety, don't I get a hug?" he says. Jeab, uniformed and hatted, hams his fists each side my door. He hugs me. "Son, I'm nipped to pieces."

Brothers.

I shove back my brother.

"But don't I even get a hug?" he says. The soldier in my doorway takes my shoulders in his hands. "You still don't see it, Bub," he says. "My heart was roped. You get it? I got sweet on Doll."

I laugh and shoot my brother dead.

Out Back

My mama's cough comes through the darkness of our hall from in her room. My mama's voice comes through our walls. Outside my window in the lighter dark, I hear her bedded noises fill the air out on our lawn. Her coughing sounds come hushing back on through my window glass to me. Her crumping mattress ticks, it pings; I hear her sounds surround my head—my mama's cough comes in my breath.

I can't remember what my dreaming was.

I remember seeing places on our farm.

My cousin Kay amongst the cows.

My brother bunks above me breathing measures in his sleep. My clothes and shelf, and desk and chair, and closet door are living things. Everything is watching in the dark. My cowboy lampshade tilts alive. I barely creep my covers off, then pour myself onto the floor. I am a night ground hunting creature haunting dark, a creaking nightmare me in clothes. Beside my mama's bedroom door, I miss the hallway's ticking wood. I miss our hall walls haunting quiet to our moonlit living room, the picture window clear and moonlight icy blue; this picture window holds our yard: our blue-white walk out to the road. Our fence line's harder stripes appear to tremble on the lawn, between the posts the faintly shifting, whitened boards. Every night-glown brighter thing, like snow, seems lit up from inside. Everybody lies asleep out on our world.

"Hello, stove."

"—Hello, ghosts hid in the walls."

I am the only human being awake, alive. I'm kind of *king* of everything, up late—with everybody sleeping.

Past our window curtain's shadow, bars of light fall through the house, and there are dimly painted bars of light like Halloween on things, light from the curtains in our kitchen, up the walls and on our floor. I drag my hand across the countertop, our vinyl kitchen chairs. Our kitchen backdoor, waiting, wants me in the dark, it seems to me. It always does. The greasy doorknob to our porch is sweating dew in water beads. The breezes stir: the sour pollen smell of grass, manure, dampness in the air. Our night-yard things out in the moonlight rise up dug out from the lawn. Our night yard gives to me its buried come-to-life: a concrete block, a boot, a rag, a mound of sand. A crawly salamander puppy slugs the grass. Every shape is rising! Our white fence line worms its posts up through the busting, grassy sod. Where cattle rubbed its waxy trunk, a dogwood bends etched in its silhouette; in black our swollen tractor tenses scowling in a hulk. Our barn and shed and silo leaning, close around our house. *Everything* seems drawing in the dark.

Everything seems larger, watching me. I could easily see our hoe stand up and peg across the field, our kitchen broom dance from the porch a clunking stick man in the night.

I'm sneaking out to see the cows again. To Darling in the darkness underneath our fence-line trees. I think of movie things and schoolgirls here, to clear my head of Doll.

My mama coughs back in our house, her tethered lungs like two gray fishes ladled cooking in her chest. I think of all the hollow, roomy dark where I was up in her. How was Jeab in Mama, in her water dished asleep? How was *he* in her, between her heart, her lungs, his blood? My brother, Jeab, was born the first while I was birthless still in heaven, perfect, looking at the earth.

No one is woken in our house, and no one knows. My brother sleeping in his bunk. Not even him.

I'm like my cow.

I slip on out into the darkness in our field to see what is.

Outside and farther in the night, our flattened field grass crusts the curving world, this flooded, moonlight Bible plane of war. There was a time before our farm was gone and rusted in the dirt. Once many Indians were here, the buried Spaniards, children, slaves. Their ghosts are horded in each twig, each blade of grass, each leaf, and every inch's pebbly, moonlit sand.

Flat blocks of floating river ice move loosely washed across the sky. Below the moon, the floating, thinner ices show.

The devil in his bed sleeps in the fire in the world.

Not even Mama bears the room for what is here—my mama cannot in her dreams begin to know. She would not know what to think. What would Daddy think were he to spot me in his lamp, or shoot me salted for a rustler at our herd out in the dark? I must be pretty awful sick, I bet— my getting into things, up late at night, my world, my life out with the cows.

I'm me alive. And kind of stronger-feeling, scared a bit, and free.

Now look out farther in this crowded field, the cow shapes gather blocked out in the dark up by the trees; my cows lie jutting black as slag, or coal, or dropped-off slabs of stone great passing ices left behind.

I move in closer by our sleeping cows, the narrow, whitened cow trails road the grass out on the ground, old school map trails from what were once my daddy's long-dead other cows. Back when my daddy was a boy, he walked our farm as poor as dirt.

We're sort of cracker still, I guess, with our few cows.

The cow pies, little baby seed cows of themselves dropped on the ground, each cow pie grows a little cowling in the dust. Their steaming breath lifts from the mud.

Our waking large, and black, and bedded, sleepy cows. Watch.

—I'm not a dog. I'm not afraid to walk on up on gentle them, nor them on me. I'm just their feed as long as I am not afraid. Some blinky cows nose at the wind of me . . . look outward on the dark, then go to sleep.

Now look here by this shadow cow!

A cow shape lies asleep with all its legs tucked under it, as if this cow were standing up but all its legs were in the ground, as if this cow stood to its belly in a mossed and solid pond, a legless water-creature cow, a mottled stone.

The grass around this cow runs lighter, glowing still. An icy cloud goes past the moon. The clouds are rising on the night.

Darling moos. Darling outside on her grassy sandlot bedded down in dark.

I whisper, "Whoa, there, Daddy's home. Hey, pumpkin."

Look at Darling black and white, a milk cow-headed shroud wrapped on a cowhide-colored tomb. A legless Bible figure cow, an idol god. Darling trunks around her head, a stiffly, bored—which sort of turns into—a spurning cow regard, turns back around. I'm not much news enough for her. She nods her nose; winks wide awake; she chews her cud.

"Hey, Sugar doll, hey, girl, hey, love . . . who is Daddy's only, special one?"

I scratch the hair sleeve on her horn-shaped, bony horns. I pat her jaw, tug at her dewlap, hanging baggy down from her. I've got to get out from my clothes and straddle horse-back onto Darling. A warmth like Mama's comes from Darling, toasty warming me to her, my pants and shirt bunched in a pillow as I saddle on her back.

This is how we are.

One night.

One late-at-night out back, with all our sleeping cows. The sitting bull. In several lazy different moves she rolls her bulk in front of her; she rears her butt into the air; she cricks her sounds of her inside her with the thick and crunkly bones. I'm riding bare-back on my Doll, naked. Darling throws her bulk behind and stretches up and stands. "Hey, easy, girl." So here we go. She coughs a throaty pull of cud and wags her ear flaps on her head. She bucks me. Darling lopes along with us—with me up bare-butt naked riding hidden in the night, a naked Indian on her. A witch, a freak.

This scene would break my mama's heart for her to see us, secret here.

Darling clops the spidered grasses. Darling moos. Jean and Mindy on their bellies, bedded, pick. Bedded Dot and Sophie pass. My dolly bobs my butt against her riding me on top of her; she bumps my butt bone on her hip pin's knuckled ridge; she eases shuddery; she cants. She rolls her gait into a smooth and shockless trot. I feel the wind rise up and play at us, on Darling loping hard as if to leave me in the night, her furrowed ribs like hayrake combs. We

gallop charged across the haunted ground—the world rocks
rolling by us as we plod into the dark. My skinny legs hold
me to her.

See how we go.

"Don't say anything to Mom about the cows," I say to Jeab.

"I used to ride you on my bike," he says. "You wasn't
but this big."

I pulled my shrinking part from her and hugged my heart
to Doll.

Outside in our boxing-ring corral, I dip my frog off in the
trough water, splash the water lappy on my legs and on my
belly. Get dressed and brush my butt and everywhere for
dust and little hairs.

I try, but I can't love with Darling.

I can't keep my mind enough from Mama in my head.

I see that everything is lighter out and tireder to me.
Every outside shape seems broken into lines. I sneak back
quiet through the yard below the windows of our house. A
plastic compound bucket, turned, spills heels of bread, potato peelings, rocks of curd. A glassy bread bag shard sits
littered on the grass. Nothing lives here anymore. Our
kitchen backdoor frames the blackness of the dark inside
our house; our house's dark seems hollowed empty, without
walls; our house's dark could stretch a hundred yards, a
field length underground, a lightless cave.

Our dim-lit living room unrolls beyond the door.

He's home.

The devil with his wings crossed, sitting, nods, his oily

road tar on our floor. "Who is Daddy's only, special love?" the devil says. He licks his tongue down at his legs, inside my head.

My mama hums and murmurs talk along our hall.

Mama knows. My mama and daddy and Jeab and Kay and everybody knows. I lie a promise I won't do this anymore. I promise God. I plan the ways that I will stop it. I won't hide. I'm through with Doll.

I tell God I want to die.

On slipping into bed I tuck my covers with my sheet wrapped on the cover's satin trim. My brother's bed sags like a coffin lid. Our old refrigerator sends its moaning motored hum. I hear my pillow pulse my head. My lifting window curtains breathe against the balmy, blowing wind; the see-through rose lace on my curtains stencil patterns on the glass. My mama's cough drifts on the air out on our land.

"Poppa, swing me next," my mama, sleepy-sounding, says.

Now I remember seeing Kay was in my dream. Our summer fields. The brushing stands of dried-up field weed flowers, straws, and leaves, and seedpod shakers, sun-curled thistle stalks. Our field burns smoking on the edges in my dream. Our trees are cloud. Are clouded, burning wads of hair lined in a smoking, fired row.

I am walking in the weeds. I'm setting fire to the field grass in the ashed and silted sun. In smoldered scrub I walk alone. Way back behind me, Mama and Daddy hoe the smoke out from the ground: it seems our fields are being burned as if for later sowing corn. My brother and Kay herd at our cows off to my side. I leave the weeds. *This* is what my nightmare dreaming was; this is what I see down on the grass: a sort of borning, baby thing dished in a blood-wet liquid sack, and dust, with peppered bits of ashes on its caul. A thing alive. A baby pig or floating cat like in a jar. It twitches clotted in the rubber of its blood—it curls its legs. I have seen this kind of thing out here before left with the calves. Its little face, a spill of matted, bluish hair in egg and inside-looking skin. A nightmare wound come off and come to life, an unbirthed baby calf. But on this unbirthed baby calf there sits a human baby's head, and on this head split little fingered nubs of horn, and there is cow hair on its skin, and little cow foot baby legs with little hooves instead of hands. I can't get my wind up in my breath. I can't but scream; my mouth is shrieking without sound, a windless scream. My mama and daddy are walking up on me with hoes. They see me kicking at the dust.

They see me try to bury it with my shoe.

They see me try to kill the thing.

"Don't say anything to Mama about the cows," I say to Jeab.

I shoot him.

Over and over and over again.

Now look out on our field across the grasses and the dust, this country. Look here through my window on our world.

I am never getting up from bed or out at night again.

I'm done.

"All right," my mama says. She coughs. "Is that you being up?"

. . .

My brother Jeab stands in my doorway going out into his life.

"So, can't you give your brother a hug?" he says, his NAVY-decaled briefcase, hat, his duffel strapped and shouldered like a rifle by my door, bottles, ripped and twisted beer cans, flakes of glass and scattered shells.

Chatter.

Squirrels run in my cupboard, birds. My Super Glued-up saucers, cups, my parrot-headed mixer spins its silver, bladed eyes. Dishes, everything stirs alive! In my refrigerator's crisper sits the head of my old cow where freezing eels and lizards breed. Rocking, light tents on my kitchen as the bulb burns on the cord lamp blurred and blue with stars of glare.

"It's true. She's all I had to want," he says. "Hell, *I* wasn't but this big."

My kitchen window holds the dawning. There are windowed chips of light out on the waking city's walls, hot beads of light like on machines, far, little lamplights on a mountain road with walkers in the dark. Small-lighted, other people's lives. The watered, palely lit-up morning dark shows shadowed buildings flatly, thinned and blackened by the daylight, flecked with checkerboards of glass. A papered shadow-someone crosses on a drawn-shut window shade, goes smaller walking from the shade, then disappears.

Another light comes on across the street: a bed, a color television. News is what I see, and someone's legs in their apartment. One red chair.

Jeab holds out his arms to me and rubs his chest to mine.

We hug. His cigaretted beer breath and the bearding on his neck. My chin rests warming at his jawbone near his ear, his orange hair, his hat strap's leather length of cool between my temple and his head.

My brother hugs his arms on me like Daddy's hugging once—his hug surrounds, sits on, and crushes me. I'm girlish in his arms, like I was Mama in his arms. Like I was Mama, or my cousin, or a calf held in his arms. His arms are huge. His hug is huge. I'm nothing serious to anyone—to Daddy, nor to Jeab. This is how my brother's hugging feels.

I just wished he'd get it over with.

So, I want Jeab to kiss me. Jeab to mount me like a dog or in our shower on the floor. I wish that I could love him, Jesus, once.

I want Jeab to go ahead and go.

My empty stairwell in the hall is like it wants someone to follow where the steps lead up my stairs, or by the stairway railing downward out my hall, it seems to me. It waits alone and wants for Jeab. Waiting, hands bend through my walls.

I rest my gun across the air to him and let its trigger click.

"You crazy shit!" is what he says.

Jeab snags his bags on down the stairs.

I pull the trigger back to snap a dot of red onto his head. Candy.

Jeab trots through my hall.

I'll shoot him.

"You come back and see us when you're able, Jeab," I say.

I'll laugh and kill my brother dead.

Brothers.

Always and over and over again.

"Bub, who do you guess had showed her? *Who was sweet on her?*" he says.

"So who was first!" Who really was?

He walks. My brother Jeab is gone.

The Fall

So I am ill a little while. I think if I can ever stop then I will hide these nights from Jeab, riding, times I take my fill hid in our shipwrecked barn with her. Then I get big. I turn thirteen, take off my mama's face for Daddy's when I lie my way with girls, my talk like rocks are in my mouth, wires, words as little bodies of the voices I will try, cotton, walking about on the air; my conning words pull from my mouth tied up in magic, knotted scarves . . . Can I remember what I saw? At times: our field out in the light. I push these nights back in my mind, but I cannot hide long from Doll.

One later day we shoot our cow is all while loading out the calves, that tiny toy-gun bit of rifle odd and sputting mad with noise. I stand and watch them put her down; there are some average nothing things that I remember in that picture—sun, a clapboard wall of light that reels reflecting from our land, the dry and raindrop-cratered sand baked with the spooning marks like moonscape from a rain the other day, our grass and fence boards, posts, and papers catching blown onto a fence, and cattle, cowbirds, road, a passing plane, gray birds high on our phone line on the blued-to-nothing sky. Separate. Everything wants us to look at it, its terribleness, the most.

Another weed, or rock, or cow horn, me, I'm there and, well, I'm not. I kind of bloat about the ground, the greening field, our brown-eyed cattle. My cousin and Mama and Daddy and Jeab and I surround in roundup style our crowded eighty head of Hereford, Brahman, Holstein milker cows. Our cows run rucksome in a dusty drove, a livestock knot of cow head, horn, and cow neck, backs, and butts. My mama and Kay are swum-in arms above the herd, my daddy and Jeab slash whips behind us; I'm a side. I gentle babies on our fence line, herding calves and counting posts.

They still are living in the world, in their old selves.

"Hup, little son. Hup, Bit, hup, girl." I drive the newborn onto Darling, watch its nose slip pink beneath its mama's swoll-up bag of milk. I herd the twins and speckled Midge. Our longhorn. Petey, Bo and Sharon, old Wynetta, Queen, and Dot, so reddish, cows of roan and ringstrakes, cows like marble, dun and cream, and in the markings of a two-tone hide I find those shapes of islands patched in licked-at black and white.

Their many tons chuck up our ground as I count sixty-seven fence posts past the ashes of our barn, our laggers loping by the footers of the barn that we will build, its skinny two-by-fours in framing, winded ash tilled in the air.

Up on the rooftop of our house sometimes, I'll catch our church's cross, a jagged mirror dot of light like broken glass out on the sky. Now there's a mall where once were cows. Some road motels and paper trailer houses, whiny, city cars.

But I remember now and then! What I remember most is not of any count if I recall, the unimportant squawking all. What I remember being mostly stuff like trashy yards and faucets, tarry gravel in our grass, a stripy shirt I've always had and, once, a night I woke to pee and saw—a second of our father, Daddy, crying in the hall.

Cattle. Bottle-sucking calves. My teddy doll I have in bed. I've got my dusty cars and army men and hand-me-downish shirts, Kay light and new inside the skin on her, the tautness of her body soft as water-polished fruit. Kay leans to let us see her body while we dream of her and work, tired. Everywhere are ashes with my cow up near to birth; she takes with calf and waters up till I cannot get hard or heart enough to put my spill in her. She wallows big with him in her, white like an egg around his boiling solid ball of yolk in her.

I trade my milking her with Jeab, and in the mornings for my work do all the feeding up instead.

I close the small me off from Kay.

I stop with Doll.

I wish I'd never seen a cow.

Across the moony, cratered planet of these hoofmarks on our land, I make believe a giant snake has made this trail behind our cattle, hellish snake that leaves its slither in a ring around the world, giant. Always I've been gone. I boot the bugs rolled in a cow pie eating mulchy balls of turd. I'm herding. I walk close to Kay; I miss our fun. "Yip, babies, come on," Mama calls. She swirls a handkerchief in circle like it tries to chase its tail, a birdish, stirring purple fan that Mama circles with her hand. Our cows come on.

I ride the merry-go-rounding gate end swinging closed, and chain the gate. We leave the baby straggle calves and baby bulls to cut, outside.

I see it all. I see the things that sit apart and babble separate there for us: an elbowed nail bent from a post, a feather knifing in the chicken wire's fencing by our shed, a flint of rock, the crockery handle of a cup thumbed from the dirt, a sun-bleached some week's page of news blown on our fence this afternoon. Our mostly skittish, dusted cattle, one big creature, in their herd.

I see her fall.

Her gentle, sweet-eyed grazing nod, our lathered musk, her tender love.

Would I have saved her if I could?

I doubt it. I'm here in my chair and watch the TV through my life.

She hollered. "Y'all come in, let's eat!" Mama said.

I went to her where he had been, and hugged our lovely cow.

Our daddy, tall, climbs our corral. He sends the curved and lazy stinger of his bullwhip on the herd, his looping pencil line of violence. Cows go wild in our corral. A crowded, stirring stew of cow flesh on the whitewashed warp of boards, a sound—potatoes from a dumptruck, from our cow lot—thunder sounds, lightning, cows all searching, circled, thick as fishes for a hole. Our outlaw longhorn leads the herd, around, around. The longhorn hooks a steer rump gotten close enough to gore. It slobbers, raking with its horns against a board to butt the air.

I watch, but I can't think at all, like I am *rock* or like the mustards pressed on white against the boards, pressed yellow flowers through the cow legs on the paint of our corral. I stop, but everything is wrong. Our crazing longhorn stops our herd. It digs its hooves as if to warn. Each cow moves schooled against the milking stalls, their cow selves rocking backwards, nodding serious and shy, then like a dog they nod to Daddy, nod to see what with his bullwhip Daddy waits for them to do. I hear a cow kick through the wood. We're cardboard. Nothing here will hold.

"Well, girls, that's it!" my daddy says. He rolls his bullwhip lassoed up and yells for Jeab to fetch his pistol from the glovebox in our truck.

I check the gate chain on the gate post, climb the ladder of our gate. I see the dipping ropes of wire on the light poles on our road, a row of twitching, iron birds sits thick and solid on our phone lines in the quiet on the air. A birdless line dips to our house.

Our quiet phone floats in the dusk of Mama's nightstand by their bed, her perfumed air blue in their bedroom, nylons, Mama's rubber bulb.

I watch as Jesus leaves his picture with the knickknacks on the wall. Our smoking ghosts move through the sofa. Ticking footsteps walk our hall.

My daddy wraps his hands about his pistol at the herd.

An empty car blows through our world.

A snap of smoke.

The birds explode, in tatters, flying off our phone line. All our cows go piling out, a surge of dun and dusty black and white in cowhide-ruptured colors through the clouded dust and air. A butted fence board cracks, is stoven in. I'm knocked back hammered flat; I'm windless, down and sucking dust and almost drowning on the ground—my eyes go tilted on our world, a dizzy turn.

Unreal, a crab leg thrash of cows kicks past the tore and scattered boards. Our nodding cows jump over the wood. My mama screams, she laughs, she lifts me, starry hands, her wanding arm. I'm baby me again, with Mama on the ocean in her arms. I feel kind of smaller, me with Mama, me and her.

One normal day we lose our milk cow. That is all.

Another time, another night, I turn the light out on our mirror, bring my face up in the closeness of my breath against the glass. Shifter, William underwater as my eyes come into light—my mirrored lives. I see my head on me made silhouette, then Daddy, Jeab, the devil, in our mirror there, instead. I see us all.

I make my face turn into mine. I make my face be like the face I've got when calm is in my mind, like when I'm vacuuming or hoeing good or praying in our tub.

I put my arm *outside myself* and reach up for the light.

I see my Doll.

Our longhorn addles through the herd of funneled cow backs thick and hillsome falling cloppy past the kindling gate. Our longhorn quits the herd and nuzzles Darling at our stall. Its horning head up in her bag, our longhorn scratches into Darling like the butting hungry calf would nuzzle Darling up for milk. It gently gores her to the ground, its longhorn nose lost under Darling, scooting cow about the sand.

It throws its horns up hefting Darling in this forklift to her knees.

My daddy's whip roars loose in air exploding dust and floating hairs.

The scattered phone-line birds reflock and fly an arc above our barn, and whirling turned in single file they settle soft back on the wires.

Darling rises.

Moos.

She falls.

Our sleepy world burns in the boredom of our normal noonlight sun.

Our normal everyday goes on, no bother, always as it does. We break for lunch I think, my family, while our cow bleeds on the sand, her snuffs of breath against the ground with little flittings of the dust up from the sand on our corral.

We sit in our kitchen. We are waiting to be fed. We have the pepper-breaded chickens, tea, and peas and greens, and sausage, Mama talking on our phone. My grandpa, Daddy, Jeab, and Kay load out our calves to take for sale.

I stay to help with who it is we call the dog man, when he comes. I figure hope at last has come. I reckon God is in his truck. The dog man's wrecker bumps our yard and wails its blatting murdered horn. I run to do for him the gate and hold it open as he drives. He yawps his horn at us again. "You all come sit awhile," shouts Grandma with her bucket from our house.

I show the dog man Darling bloated on the sand. A slick of oil tars her ground. She founders swollen as a plum.

"She's sucking wind is what it is," he sisses, rolling with a bottle cap like candy on his tongue. He sucks the corkside of it in like he has swallowed whole a bottle with the top poked from his mouth. The printed cap reads spitted wet.

"You looky. Watch her gobble air."

He stares at Darling on the sand, his one eye roaming from our cow. He sucks the cap into his lungs, and like to test a rotting porchstep, toes his boot into her ribs.

Darling

"We've got to let her air out some," the dog man, toeing Darling, says.

The dog man, giggly, slides his rifle from the gun rack in his truck. He gnaws and comes with toothy rattles, muddled words warped from his mouth.

She coughed. "Is that you being up?" she said.

He rests his toy on Darling's chest.

She moos her breath to us.

He fires.

Darling's air in her goes wheezing on our land.

I shoot him dead. I plug the slug into my brother. Could have. Times I come to think of him, I'll kill my brother Jeab. I'll see it. Then I'm sick with love.

I'll think, If I can't blast my brother, maybe I could die instead, or Daddy. Mama at her roses as the dew taps from the gate.

He took her. She was always his.

After this, my father brings his face up from my mind. I grow to look like I am him, and wax my face formed into Daddy's, molting. Surfacing into my father where he lives within my skin, a surge of *him* come into life. My father, Dad, around my eyes.

I think that I remember how the light is in the sky. I maybe do. Or maybe it is just another day. I'm in a lean up to the gate post with my cheek against my hands, our crummy world awash in brightness, hot and awful, average made. I see the spirits in the air, the thoughtful rocks and trees and tatter. I see trash dragged in our yard. I stand to keep the dogs from her, her puddle, standing there and staring. Darling's head logged on the sand.

Up close I touch the freckled eye, drying. All I am is chalk.

Standing, this is what I see as I am looking through the air: a racing shadow of a plane skates on our land to mar our yard, it frets the fence boards on the stall and skims the sand on our corral—a blink of darkness shades my skin. I'm made a shadow, tinted dim an instant, blue, then it is gone.

A sun-blind white is what the sky is overhead, a Southern sky. My eyes see white, then black, then red blurred at the sky to find the plane—its sound, like ocean or a highway, roaded car rush in our air, and there it is. This flying arrowtip of tiny, silver, irritating nail, a far-off plane toyed in the air with all its speck-size seated people at their windows from the world.

I dream of places on the world like on a ball. I think of towns mapped on the globe with all those lives lived in my mind.

They leave us, me alone with Darling and her cow shit on the sand. I drop and touch the heat from her, petting.

I'm already gone. I have no *me* up in my body, cut and gutted like the cat we did in science class—I'm shelled, reamed open, raw back to my bones, a bluing stack of eaten crabs.

I called her.

"Come on, girl. Come on."

A running color of the shadow of the plane across our land, I watch, I watch as they are flying, Kay, my brother in the air, small as a miracle in there where I have conjured up their lives, like Doll, the painted china horse that trots the gray inside my mind, perfect, lazing with me in my sleep, in grass, imagined as a memory, a calling up of her body by our greenly shading trees. I see the names that I have lost—those hearts: our ghostly linen cattle, coal or pottery red or white, or grazing idly in their brilliance giving calm up to our breeze, or shimmering, combed inside and honeyed as the beeman's hive with cream, like grace, in stillness by the fencing, by the stony, sea green wreckage of a truck hulled on the field. I see the times I've had with us tucked from the cloud-hid attic lightning, rainy days about her stall, longing, lolling around in the blondeness of our flowery hay and heat, see then my brother's later lives, my cousin Kay around him coupling legged in love up in their plane, like Doll and I up in a dream at night, the cords to hold our bodies kiting light above the earth, our tiny, imitation lives. My heart! Two idiots in flight above our world up near the sun, up in the places in the world where lovers go.

I rode her.

"Come on, love," I called.

The Blue Rooms

My mother lifts me up off of the grass. She crooks my head up and lowers my butt so I can see what all there is here in the glare around our house, a sunned and cartoon-wobbly, dewed-on farm, our monstrous pigs and chickens scribbling clawmarks in their dust, like deserts, tiny hills and islands on the map across our yard, and the green beyond. A Canaan, wilderness and shadow is the forests of our corn. The awful Babel of our silo, barn, our restless legging bushes, fence and fruit trees lawned in grass, each thing too rawly bright to look at, gleaming, things that all but sing I witness one-thing-at-a-time. Each thing sits blazing like our bushes, live with color, wet with light. The leeky greenness of our trees, the belling lemon yellow pears. Our fence, a bone white on the daylight, powdered sky.

Our cow is there.

I choke, my chest bloats up with cough, my one bare sock out on the air, in Mama's arms.

She takes her child on to our house whisked through the yard grass with a whisper, past the lipped and open roses with their wounds around our gate to the shadowed lawn.

My mother scoops my shoe where I have lost it on the

grass. She bends us up and snuggly cups it huffing wind about my foot, and shifting hold of me to hug her, Mama takes us from the sun, to shadows; softly weighted sounds squawk from the darkness of our house (I knew that this is how the world would end: the television on).

And so we go—she takes me up our shaking steps. She carries me in, the way they'd take his F-18 on the carrier deck, to iron, out of heaven, lowered dark into the stowage—bits of air still there in currents of the world against my arms—and so she takes me on inside, from brilliant light into the shade, into the underwater blueness of the dark inside our house. My mother shuffles us up the shaded porch and cradles me on inside our house into our average lives.

And see how Darling holds the light in this same field out in our world?

I see her small out in my window. Doll and I.

Lovers.

We were all there was.

I load my gun and crack a beer and go back dead into my bed. I make her body in my mind. I try, but I can't hold the picture. Almost every night that passes, I remember less of her.

A NOTE ABOUT THE AUTHOR

WILLIAM TESTER IS A NATIVE OF SOUTH CAR-
OLINA, AND NOW LIVES IN NEW YORK CITY. THIS
IS HIS FIRST WORK OF FICTION.

A NOTE ON THE TYPE

THE TEXT OF THIS BOOK WAS SET IN SABON,
A TYPE FACE DESIGNED BY JAN TSCHICHOLD
(1902–1974), THE WELL-KNOWN GERMAN TY-
POGRAPHER. BECAUSE IT WAS DESIGNED IN
FRANKFURT, SABON WAS NAMED FOR THE FA-
MOUS FRANKFURT TYPE FOUNDER JACQUES
SABON, WHO DIED IN 1580 WHILE MANAGER
OF THE EGENOLFF FOUNDRY. BASED LOOSELY
ON THE ORIGINAL DESIGNS OF CLAUDE GARA-
MOND (C. 1480–1561), SABON IS UNIQUE IN
THAT IT WAS EXPLICITLY DESIGNED FOR HOT-
METAL COMPOSITION ON BOTH THE MONOTYPE
AND LINOTYPE MACHINES AS WELL AS FOR FILM
COMPOSITION.

COMPOSED BY PENNSET, INC.,
BLOOMSBURG, PENNSYLVANIA

PRINTED AND BOUND BY
THE HADDON CRAFTSMEN,
SCRANTON, PENNSYLVANIA

DESIGNED BY GEORGE J. MCKEON